"Maybe I can help." Sloan motioned to her daughter.

"She doesn't go to strangers," Maggie said.

"It's worth a try." He held out his arms. "Hey, Shorty, what's up?"

The little girl silently stared at him, probably didn't know what to make of a man in the kitchen. Maggie braced for an ear-splitting protest, but after a moment's hesitation, Danielle went to him and settled her chubby little arm around his neck.

Maggie's heart melted at the sight of the big man carrying her little girl.

Gorgeous, charming and good with kids. Sloan Holden was a triple threat. But he must have a flaw.

Every man did.

* * *

THE BACHELORS OF BLACKWATER LAKE:
They won't be single for long!

D0174022

Dear Reader,

This is book number nine set in the fictional town of Blackwater Lake, Montana. When the series started, Maggie Potter was only briefly mentioned. In subsequent stories, I spent more time with her and watched her personality grow stronger until it became clear that she needed her own book.

The Doctor and the Single Mom was Maggie's series debut, and she'd recently lost her soldier husband in Afghanistan and was pregnant. In *One Night with the Boss*, she encouraged her brother to take a chance on love, and he did. It was just wrong for Maggie not to find love, too. So *The Widow's Bachelor Bargain* is for her.

Since we last saw Maggie, she's been busy raising her daughter and expanding her ice cream parlor business to include a café. To help pay for the loan that made the expansion possible, she turns her house into a B and B, renting a room to Sloan Holden, who's in Blackwater Lake to work on the new resort his company is building.

Sloan has been quoted as saying he wasn't very good at being a husband and will never marry again, although many women are willing to try to change the millionaire's mind. But Maggie isn't like many women and refuses to risk her heart again. Still, the roomies find it's only a matter of time until their bargain to not complicate the situation with personal feelings is compromised with, well, personal feelings.

Prominently displayed in my office is a sign that says Happily Ever After, and I take the responsibility very seriously. Maggie has a special place in my heart, and I hope you enjoy her story.

Happy reading!

Teresa Southwick

The Widow's Bachelor Bargain

Teresa Southwick

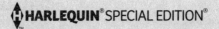
HARLEQUIN® SPECIAL EDITION®

Recycling programs
for this product may
not exist in your area.

ISBN-13: 978-0-373-65933-3

The Widow's Bachelor Bargain

Copyright © 2016 by Teresa Southwick

Printed in U.S.A.

Teresa Southwick lives with her husband in Las Vegas, the city that reinvents itself every day. An avid fan of romance novels, she is delighted to be living out her dream of writing for Harlequin.

To the men and women
of the United States Armed Forces and their
families. Your sacrifices have ensured our freedom,
and I am forever in your debt.

Chapter One

"You must be Mr. Holden. And—happily—you're not a serial killer."

Sloan Holden expected beautiful women to come on to him, but as pickup lines went, that one needed tweaking. He stared at the woman, who'd just opened the door to him. "Okay. And you know this how?"

"I had you investigated." Standing in the doorway of her log cabin home turned bed-and-breakfast, Maggie Potter held up her hand in a time-out gesture. "Wait. I'm a little new at this hospitality thing. Delete what I just said and insert welcome to Potter House. Please come in."

"Thanks." He walked past her and heard the door close. Turning, he asked, "So, FBI? CIA? DEA? NSA? Or Homeland Security?"

"Excuse me?"

"Which alphabet-soup agency did you get to check me out?"

"Actually, it was Hank Fletcher, the sheriff here in Blackwater Lake. I apologize for blurting that out. Guess I'm a little nervous. The thing is, I live here with my two-year-old daughter and another, older, woman who rents a room. It's my responsibility to check out anyone who will be living here."

Sloan studied the woman—Maggie Potter—dressed in jeans and a T-shirt covered by a pink-and-gray-plaid flannel shirt. Her shiny dark hair was pulled back into a ponytail and her big brown eyes snapped with intelligence and self-deprecating humor. She was pretty in a wholesome, down-to-earth way, and for some reason that surprised him. He'd assumed the widow renting out a room would be frumpy, silver haired and old enough to be his grandmother. It was possible when his secretary had said *widow*, he'd mentally inserted all the stereotypes.

"Still," he said, sliding his hands into his jeans' pockets, "a serial killer by definition gets away with murder and is clever enough to hide it. Maybe I'm hiding something."

"Everyone does. That just makes you human." The wisdom in that statement seemed profound for someone so young. "But you, Mr. Sloan Holden, can't even spit on the sidewalk without someone taking a picture. I doubt you could ditch photographers long enough to pull off a homicide, let alone hide the incriminating evidence."

"You're right about that."

"Even so, Hank assured me you are who you say you are and an upstanding businessman who won't stiff me for the rent. Again I say welcome." She smiled, and the effect was stunning. "I'll do everything possible to make your stay here as pleasant as possible, Mr. Holden."

"Please call me Sloan."

"Of course." When she turned away, he got a pretty good look at her work-of-art backside and shapely legs. They weren't as long as he usually liked, but that didn't stop all kinds of ideas on *how* to make his stay pleasant from popping into his mind. That was proof, as if he needed more, that he was going to hell. After all, she was a mother.

"I just need you to sign the standard guest agreement." She walked over to the desk in the far corner of the great room.

Sloan followed and managed to tear his gaze away from her butt long enough to get a look at her home. A multi-colored braided rug was the centerpiece for a conversation area facing the fireplace. It consisted of a brown leather sofa and a fabric-covered chair and ottoman. On the table beside it was a brass lamp and a photo of Maggie snuggled up to a smiling man. Must be the husband she'd lost.

Maggie handed over a piece of paper and he glanced through it, the normal contract regarding payment responsibilities, what was provided, dos and don'ts. He took the pen she handed him and signed his name where indicated.

"Do you need a credit card and ID?" That was standard procedure for a hotel.

"I recognize you from the magazines you seem to be in on a weekly basis. And I got all the pertinent financial information from your secretary. Elizabeth says you'll be staying in town for a while to work on the resort project."

"That's right."

"I know you're here at Potter House because Blackwater Lake Lodge had a major flood when a pipe burst and is now undergoing repairs and renovations. Elizabeth told me you do a lot of work outside the office and wouldn't be happy with all the pounding, hammering and drilling."

"She knows me well."

"I got that impression. And she said you're not a heartless jerk like most tabloid stories make you out to be."

"Did I mention she's loyal?"

He folded his arms over his chest and studied her. Elizabeth was the best assistant he'd ever had and an impeccable judge of character, even on the phone. She wasn't in the habit of sharing details about him. Not that she'd given away secrets to a competitor, but still… While taking care of his living arrangements for this stay in Blackwater Lake, Montana, she must have phone-bonded with Maggie Potter, meaning that she trusted this woman.

In any event, he didn't have a lot of choice about where to hang his hat. The lack of accommodations in this area, along with a beautiful lake and spectacular mountains, were the very reasons this resort project he and his cousin Burke had undertaken would be a phenomenal financial success. It was their luck that no one else had noticed the amazing potential of this area before now.

"It sounds as if you got to know my assistant pretty well," he finally said.

"Lovely woman. She invited me to her wedding."

"Wow. You really did make a good phone impression. I didn't even get an invitation," he teased.

"She's probably concerned that the kind of photographers who follow you around aren't the ones she wants documenting the most important day of her life."

Sloan knew she was joking, but that wasn't far from the truth. Because he had money, his every move seemed to generate a ridiculous amount of public interest—make that *female* interest. That would give a guy trust issues even if he hadn't been burned, but Sloan was a wealthy divorced bachelor and deliberately never stayed with the same woman for more than a couple of months.

A man in his position had social obligations and often needed a plus one. On the surface it looked like dating, but he knew it was never going anywhere. So the more women he went out with, the more interest his personal life generated. But he was ultimately an entrepreneur who knew getting his name in the paper was a positive. Even bad publicity could be good.

And interest continued to escalate about whether or not any woman could catch the most eligible bachelor who had said in more than one interview that he would never get married again. That it just wasn't for him. The remark, intended to snuff out attention, had really backfired on him and created the ultimate challenge for single women looking for a rich husband. He was like the love lottery.

"My assistant knows I'd never let anything spoil her special day."

"Because you respect the sanctity of marriage so much?" It sounded as if there was the barest hint of sarcasm in her question.

He didn't doubt that she knew the tabloid version of his disastrous foray into matrimony. It was well documented and also ancient history. "I do for other people," he answered sincerely.

"Just not for yourself."

"It's always good to know your own limitations."

"Seems smart. And wise," she agreed. "So how long will you be here?"

"Indefinitely." That was certainly an indefinite answer. "I handle the construction arm of the company, so it will probably be quite a while. And Blackwater Lake Lodge is undergoing renovations."

"True."

He glanced around and found he liked the idea of not living in a hotel for what would probably be months. "You have a nice place here."

"Thanks. My husband built it." There was fierce pride in her voice even as a shadow slid into her eyes. "It wasn't planned as a bed-and-breakfast. We opened a business in town."

"Oh?"

"Potter's Ice Cream Parlor on Main Street."

He nodded. "I saw it on my way here."

"Danny, my husband—" she glanced at the picture and

a softness slipped into her eyes "—thought everything through. Downstairs is the master bedroom with another room for a nursery. But he figured as the kids got older, into their teens, they'd need their privacy—bedrooms and separate baths. And a game room to hang out in. There's even an outside entrance for the upstairs. I'm not quite sure how he planned to deal with that when they were teenagers." She shrugged and the light dimmed in her dark eyes. "It didn't work out as he planned, but it works for my needs now."

He wouldn't have asked if she hadn't brought it up. And he probably shouldn't have asked anyway, but the question came out before he could stop it. "What *are* your needs?"

A slight narrowing of her eyes told him she didn't miss the double entendre, though he hadn't meant it that way. She answered the question directly. "I decided to expand the ice cream parlor to include a café, a little more healthy and upscale than a coffee shop. Even though I took on a partner, we needed an infusion of capital. The simple answer is that I need the money to pay back the business loan."

"I see."

"Josie, my other boarder, has been here for a few months. I've known her for a long time and this arrangement works for her. She's a widow and doesn't want the responsibility of a big house. When she wants to travel, she can go without worrying about the house she left behind. For the other room, you're my first. Tenant, I mean." A becoming flush crept into her cheeks. "Someone from your company who knows my brother contacted him about your housing dilemma and he put them in touch with me."

"And still you investigated me." One corner of his mouth curved up.

"It never hurts to be cautious."

Sloan couldn't argue with her about that. "So who is your brother?"

"Brady O'Keefe."

"Hmm."

She frowned. "Do you know him?"

"Not personally. But I know the name. He did some computer and website work for my company."

Sloan also knew the guy was pretty well off. The way Maggie had emphasized the word *need* when talking about money, he was pretty certain her brother hadn't been involved in raising the capital to expand her business.

"You look puzzled about something, Sloan."

"I am. But it's none of my business."

"Probably not." She shrugged. "Ask anyway."

He nodded. "I know your brother by reputation and he has a few bucks. Yet you didn't get the expansion loan from him."

One of her eyebrows rose. "How do you know that?"

"Because you said you *need* money to pay back the loan. I don't think your brother would pressure you or put you and his niece out on the street if you fell behind on payments."

"No." She smiled. "But I wanted to do this on my own. My way."

"And what way is that?" *Not the easy way*, Sloan thought.

She glanced at the photograph, then back at him. "When Danny and I opened the ice cream parlor, Brady wanted to help us, but my husband refused. He appreciated the offer, but it was important to him to do it on his own. A respect thing. Some might call it macho male pride."

"I see."

"He said it was human nature for people to not appreciate things they didn't have to work hard for. So we poured our heart, soul, blood, sweat and tears into the project.

Our phase one. The plan was always to expand and open the café, but there was a setback when he was killed in Afghanistan."

"I'm sorry." Stupid words. So automatic and useless. Why wasn't there something to say that would actually help?

"Thank you." She slid her fingers into her jeans' pockets. "Danny's gone, so I'm carrying on the dream. The way he would have wanted—without my brother's help."

"With three sisters, I can say with certainty that my instinct would be to write a check if they needed it. Brady probably feels that way, too. So how's he taking this loan thing?"

"You'd think I gave his computer a particularly nasty virus." She grinned. "Still, I think he's secretly proud of me."

Sloan didn't doubt that. What brother wouldn't be proud of a sister like her? It would have been easy to let herself be taken care of after losing her husband, but she hadn't. She was raising their child and running an expanded business plus taking in boarders. Doing things her way. And it was a good way.

She glanced at his empty hands. "I assume you have luggage. I'll show you to your room, then bring your things up."

"Thanks, but I'll get everything." His way wasn't to let a woman carry his stuff, especially when that woman looked as if the first stiff breeze would blow her away. He admired her independence, but he did things his way, too. "There's a lot and some of it is heavy."

"Okay. Follow me."

Now, *that* he didn't mind doing, because she had an exceptionally fine backside. Aside from her obvious external attributes, there was a lot to like about his new landlady.

Smart, straightforward, self-reliant. Salt of the earth. He would bet his last dime that she wasn't a gold digger.

He almost wished she was.

The next morning Maggie settled her crabby daughter in the high chair beside the round oak kitchen table. After giving the little girl a piece of banana, she whipped up a batch of biscuits and popped them in the oven. When the idea had taken hold to rent out the upstairs rooms, she'd come up with a different breakfast menu for each day of the week. Today was scrambled eggs with spinach, mushrooms, onion and tomato. Fried potatoes. Country gravy for the biscuits. And blueberries. This was one of Josie's favorites and made one wonder how the older woman stayed so trim. Could have something to do with her being tall and the brisk walk she took every morning after rolling out of bed.

Maggie hadn't seen Sloan yet this morning and was just the tiniest bit curious about what his favorite breakfast was and how he stayed in such good shape. The snug T-shirt he'd had on when checking in yesterday had left little to the imagination, and the man had a serious six-pack going on. Ever since she'd opened the door, her nerves had been tingling, some kind of spidey sense. It was like the princess-and-the-pea story she read to Danielle. Even when he wasn't near, she *knew* he was under her roof.

He wasn't model handsome, but there was something compelling in his eyes, which were light brown with flecks of green and gold.

"Mama—" The single word was followed by the sound of a splat.

Maggie looked up from stirring the country gravy and saw that Danielle had thrown her banana on the floor. Very little had been ingested, but the little girl had mangled the fruit pretty well.

"Want some Cheerios, sweetie?"

"Cookie—"

Some words came out of this child's mouth as mangled as that banana, but *cookie* wasn't one of them. It was tempting to give in and let her have a treat. Just this once keep her happy so the first breakfast with their VIP guest would go smoothly and convince him she knew what she was doing in the B and B business. But her maternal instincts told her that was a bad habit to start.

"Good morning." Josie walked into the kitchen freshly showered after her exercise. She was in her early sixties but looked at least ten years younger, in spite of her silver hair. The pixie cut suited her. She moved beside the high chair. "How are you, munchkin?"

The little girl babbled unintelligible sounds, which were no doubt a list of grievances about her mother being the food police.

"She's not her sunny little self today," Maggie apologized. "She was restless last night. Teething, I think. I hope she didn't disturb you."

"Not a bit. The insulation in these walls is amazing." She looked around, blue eyes brimming with understanding. "How can I help?"

"Go relax with a cup of coffee. You're a guest."

"Oh, please. We both know I'm your friend more than a paying customer. Besides the discount I get for emergency babysitting, it's a blessing to still be useful when you're as old as I am." She put a hand on her hip. "Now, what can I do?"

"You're doing it. Being a godsend." Maggie turned on the gas burner underneath the stainless-steel frying pan filled with potatoes. "If you could give Danielle a handful of that cereal, I'd be forever in your debt."

"Done." She grabbed the box from the pantry and did as requested. "Now I can get the eggs ready to scramble."

"Maybe I should change things up." Maggie grinned. "You know the menu by heart."

"How many eggs are you thinking with Sloan here? A man like that could be a big eater."

"So you met him?"

"Last night. We watched TV together in the upstairs game room. Some house-flipping program." The older woman opened the refrigerator and removed the containers of veggies that had been cut up the night before.

Maggie hadn't cooked breakfast for a man since the morning she'd said goodbye to her husband, before he deployed to Afghanistan. It wasn't the first time she'd made sure he ate before leaving the house but she'd never considered it would be her last meal with him. She'd never been able to decide whether or not she would have made the food more special if she'd known. Or if the not knowing had made the ordinary a final blessing.

"I think eight should be enough," Maggie said.

She couldn't remember how many Danny would have eaten and felt guilty about that. Every time she realized the recollections were getting fuzzier, she felt disloyal to his memory.

"With all the rest of the food," she continued, "it should be more than enough. If there are leftovers, I'll put some on a tortilla later and call it lunch."

"Okay." Josie started cracking eggs into a bowl. "He sure is a good-looking man."

"Who's that?"

"Your new boarder. Sloan. Unless there's another man you're hiding under the bed."

Just the sound of his name made Maggie's heart skip a beat. "I suppose he wouldn't have to wear a bag over his head in public."

"Not to be insensitive, Maggie. After all, I'm a widow, too. Also not blind. Take it from me, a man who looks like he does would have an almost nun thinking twice about taking final vows. You can't tell me you didn't notice."

"Of course I did." And even if she were blind, there would be no way not to notice the gravelly sex appeal lingering in his deep voice. "But you watched TV with him. What was that like?"

"He's not just a pretty face. I can tell you that. Seems to know his stuff and, quite frankly, he took a lot of the joy and mystery out of what those TV construction guys do."

"So it was like watching a medical show with a doctor who tells you how they're doing CPR all wrong?"

"Exactly." Josie grinned. "Still, he seems like a nice man. I wouldn't believe all that stuff about him in the tabloids."

"I sort of liked that story about him owning houses all over the world and swimming naked with the model."

"It does give one an image," Josie admitted.

"Did you ask him? Hanging out watching a house-flipping show seems like the perfect time to find out what inquiring minds want to know."

"It didn't occur to me, what with him talking about all the ways those TV guys could have reduced waste, pollution and environmental degradation."

A piercing wail from the high chair interrupted the fascinating conversation. What Josie had just said made Maggie even more curious than she'd already been, but now wasn't the time to pursue it. Danielle needed attention.

"Are you thirsty, baby girl?" She grabbed a sippy cup from the cupboard and filled it with milk. She handed it to her daughter, who eagerly stuck the spout in her mouth and drank. "So he's a green builder?"

"Who?" There was a twinkle in Josie's blue eyes as she stirred up eggs, veggies and seasoning in a bowl.

"Sloan. Unless there's a man *you're* hiding under the bed, Miss—"

"Good morning."

That gravelly, deep, sexy voice belonged to the man they'd just been talking about. Maggie exchanged a guilty glance with Josie but couldn't manage to come up with anything to say to him.

The sippy cup hit the wooden floor, interrupting the awkward silence. Maggie quickly stirred the potatoes before hurrying to her daughter, who was starting to squirm against the belt holding her in. Along with the high-pitched whining, it was clear the little girl wanted out. Maggie undid the strap and lifted the child from the high chair then tried to put her down. Danielle was having none of that and the screech kicked up a notch.

Please, not today, little one, Maggie silently begged. The man was accustomed to five-star hotels, and a two-year-old's temper tantrum wasn't the optimal way to put their best foot forward.

"Mommy has to finish cooking breakfast," she whispered. But Danielle shook her head and clung for all she was worth.

"I'll take her." Josie walked over with her arms outstretched, but the little girl buried her face against Maggie's shoulder.

She looked at Sloan. "I'm really sorry about this. I'll get her settled down and food will be on the table in no time."

"There's no rush. Although I'd love some coffee."

"It's made. I'll just put some in a carafe and you can

have it in the dining room. Cups and saucers are already out—"

"A mug is fine." He walked over to the coffeemaker and grabbed one of the mugs hanging from an under-the-cupboard hook. After pouring the steaming dark liquid, he blew on it, then took a sip. "Good."

Danielle had lifted her head at the sound of the deep voice and was intently studying the stranger. Her uncle Brady visited regularly, but other than him, a man in this house was a rare occurrence.

Maggie tried to put the little girl down again and got another strong, squealing protest. "Well, it's not the first time I've cooked with this little girl on my hip, and it probably won't be the last."

"Maybe I can help." Sloan set his mug on the granite island beside them and held out his arms.

"She doesn't go to strangers," Maggie said.

"It's worth a try." He held out his arms. "Hey, Shorty, what's up?"

The little girl silently stared at him, probably didn't know what to make of a man in the kitchen. Maggie braced for an earsplitting protest, but after a moment's hesitation, Danielle went to him and settled her chubby little arm around his neck. Then she touched the collar of his white cotton shirt. Obviously the man had a way with women of all ages. The shock had Maggie blinking at him, until she remembered that her daughter's hands were unwashed and still grubby.

"Oh, no—she's dirty. I'll get a washcloth—"

Sloan looked down at the banana streaks on his white shirt and shrugged. "Don't worry about it."

"I'll wash it for you."

"Whatever." He grinned when the child put her hands on his face and turned it to look at her. "You rang?"

She pointed in the general direction of the backyard. "Go 'side?"

Sloan met Maggie's gaze. "Is it okay if I take her out?"

"You don't have to—"

"I know. But I wouldn't have offered if I didn't want to. Is it all right with you?"

"Yes," she said helplessly.

"Okay, then. Let's go, Shorty."

Maggie's heart melted at the sight of the big man carrying her little girl out of the room.

"I don't remember any story in the tabloids about him having kids," Josie said. "But he sure is good with yours."

"I noticed."

Charming, good with kids and not hard on the eyes. Sloan Holden was a triple threat. But he must have a flaw. Every man did.

Chapter Two

In Sloan's opinion, Danielle Potter was the spitting image of her mother, minus the wariness in her big brown eyes. Or maybe it was sadness. Losing a husband must have been rough, especially the part where she was raising a child on her own. He set the little girl down on the patio and her feet had barely touched the ground before she headed for the grass, still wet with morning dew. It was early March, not quite spring, and a bit chilly. But the sun was shining in a clear blue sky that promised a beautiful day ahead.

He'd never before been responsible for a child. Ever. How hard could it be? Glancing around the big yard made him glad it was fenced in and the wrought iron bars were too close together for the toddler to squeeze through. He knew because that was the first thing she tried. After a quick check, he was satisfied that the gates on either side were secure and there would be no escape that way.

Sloan watched her squat and touch something with her tiny, probing finger. Bug? Snake? In two long strides he was beside her. "Whatcha got there, Shorty?"

She pointed to something he couldn't see and a stream of unintelligible sounds came out of her mouth. The expression on her face said she was looking for an appropriate response from him, but he had nothing. That happened when the party with whom you were conversing spoke a foreign language known only to herself, and possibly her mother.

"Is it grass?" He looked closer, hoping there was no dangerous, venomous creature lurking that would force him to do something manly, like deal with it.

She shook her head, then stood and toddled over to an area with bushes surrounded by bark chips to set it off from the grass. He was almost sure he'd heard somewhere that bugs collected in this environment, and it seemed like a bad idea to let her continue to explore unchaperoned.

Glancing around, he saw a brightly colored swing set with a slide and climbing equipment all rolled into one. Clearly it was there for Danielle's pleasure, so maybe he could channel her attention in that direction. And away from insect central.

He scooped her up in his arms, which set off instant rebellion. Sloan's response to this was a revelation. Size and strength were on his side and ought to count for something but really didn't. He would give her anything she wanted to make her happy.

"Want to go on the slide?" He held her high above him, pleased when she giggled. "I'll take that as a yes."

He set her at the top of the thing. It wasn't that high, but he was loath to let go and give her over to the unpredictability of gravity. It was remarkably astonishing to him how powerful his urge was to protect this small girl he'd voluntarily taken responsibility for. He held on to her as she slid down the short slide, then helped steady her at the bottom.

"Again," she said very clearly.

"Okay. And we have a winner." The sense of accomplishment he experienced at pleasing her wasn't all that dissimilar from the satisfaction he felt at overcoming a particularly challenging construction problem.

Sloan set her at the top of the structure and held on a little more loosely this time, although he was ready to scoop her up if the situation went south. Fortunately it didn't.

She grinned up at him and said, "Again."

"Your wish is my command, milady."

But before he could lift her up, the back door opened and Maggie stood there.

"Mama. Cookie," Danielle said, toddling over to her mother.

"Breakfast first." She met his gaze and there was a dash of respect in hers. "It's ready. Thanks to you for entertaining her."

"The pleasure was mine." He truly meant that. "I enjoyed hanging out with her."

"You're very good with her. Do you spend a lot of time with kids?"

"Actually, no. That was a first for me," he admitted.

"So you're a natural. Someone should alert the paparazzi," she teased.

"Oh, please no. I'll give you anything to keep my secret."

"You might change your mind after breakfast. And you must be starving. Everything is on the dining room table. Help yourself." She grabbed up her daughter and settled the child on her hip. "I'll get this one fed in the kitchen. So you can have some peace and quiet. If you're interested, I've set out newspapers—local and national."

"Thanks." Sloan was less interested in newsprint than he was the sight in front of him—the beautiful young mother snuggling her rosy-cheeked toddler close.

He understood her struggle to make a home for boarders while carving out a private space for her own family, but would rather have filled a plate and followed the two of them to the kitchen.

That was different.

An hour later, after changing out of his banana-slimed shirt into a clean one, Sloan drove into the parking lot of the O'Keefe Building, where his cousin Burke had rented office space. Maggie's brother, Brady, had built the place for his tech company's corporate office. At this point there was more room than he needed for his business, so he leased out the extra space. Sloan figured since he'd be working under the same roof as Brady, their paths would cross, and he was looking forward to meeting Maggie's brother.

Having visited on more than one occasion, Sloan knew where his cousin's office was located. After pushing the button for the correct floor, he rode the elevator up. The car stopped and the doors opened into a spacious waiting area. There was a reception desk straight ahead where Burke's assistant, Lydia, normally sat. She wasn't there now, so he walked over to the closed door, knocked once, then went inside.

"Hey, Burke, I—"

Sloan stopped dead in his tracks. His cousin was there, all right, holding a beautiful brunette in his arms while kissing her soundly. He recognized the lady. Sydney McKnight, Burke's fiancée. The scene in front of him was different from the usual all-work-all-the-time environment, and Sloan was beginning to wonder if he'd taken a tumble down the rabbit hole. His morning had started off with him entertaining a two-year-old before breakfast—not what normally happened in the five-star hotels he frequented, although not altogether objectionable, either. He'd been complimented on everything from his business expertise to the length of his eyelashes. But never had a flattering remark pleased him more than Maggie saying he was good with kids.

Now he'd accidentally intruded on a private moment. Instead of looking embarrassed, Burke proudly held on to his woman and grinned.

"Sloan," he said, "welcome to Blackwater Lake. You know Sydney."

"I do." He closed the door and moved closer to the desk, a little surprised his cousin hadn't brushed aside all the files and paperwork to have Sydney right there. Then again, Burke was a professional and would never do anything to compromise his employees or the woman he loved…no matter how much the intense expression in his blue eyes said he wanted her. "Hi, Syd."

"Sloan." She managed to wriggle out of Burke's arms and stood beside him, her cheeks a becoming shade of pink. "How are you?"

"Fine." Mostly. But he was feeling a little weird about this encounter and not entirely sure why. "Do I need to ask how you two are?"

"Spectacular," Sydney said, gazing up with love in her eyes at the man next to her, then back to him. "Very glad to see you."

"I doubt that," Sloan said, "but I'll play. Why are you glad to see me?"

"My reasons are purely selfish." She shrugged.

"You mean, it has nothing to do with you pining after me?" he teased.

"Sorry." She glanced up at her fiancé. "With you here, Burke will have help shouldering the workload and maybe have more time for me."

"Ah."

"You know if I were single I'd do it for you, cuz." Burke

looked and sounded like the soul of innocence, but it was an act.

"You're full of it." Sloan met his cousin's gaze. "But because I like Sydney, I'm happy to pick up any slack so the two of you can have couple time."

"Family time, really," Burke amended. "We try to include Liam as much as possible."

Sloan knew Burke and his son, Liam, had been through a rough patch when they moved to Blackwater Lake. Syd had been a bridge over troubled waters. But that had worked both ways when Burke had helped to convince her widower dad that she didn't have to be settled in a relationship before he could move on with his life. As it happened, the two of them had ended up falling in love and Burke had proposed a couple of months ago at her father's wedding to Loretta Goodson, the mayor of Blackwater Lake, Montana.

"How's Liam adjusting?" Sloan asked.

"Great." Burke looked thoughtful. "He's got friends. He's playing sports and doing well in school."

"That's good to hear." Sloan heard an edge to the words and hoped no one else had. It wasn't that he begrudged his cousin's happiness, but this whole perfect-life, happily-ever-after thing was starting to make his teeth hurt.

"Well," Syd said, "I have to get to work. My boss is very demanding."

Sloan knew she worked for her dad at the family-owned garage in downtown Blackwater Lake. Even if he hadn't, her khaki pants and matching shirt with a McKnight Automotive logo on the pocket would have been a clue.

Burke leaned down and kissed her lightly on the mouth. "Have a great day. Say hi to your dad for me."

"Will do." She walked to the door. "See you later, Sloan."

"Right. 'Bye, Syd."

When they were alone, he sat in one of the chairs facing his cousin's desk. "She's too good for you, Burke."

"Don't tell her that. I want to pull the wool over her eyes until we're married and she's stuck with me." He stared longingly at the door where she'd disappeared. "All I can do is my damnedest every day to be the best man I can be and make her happy."

If he had any doubts about his cousin's commitment to Sydney, they would have disappeared at the lovelorn expression on his face. Sloan had mixed feelings. On one hand, he was very glad to see Burke so happy. On the other, he knew this signaled the end of any bachelor-type fun with his best friend.

And suddenly it hit him what had been bothering him since walking in on Syd and Burke. He felt as if he was on the outside looking in. Alone. Lonely and a little bit envious. What a shallow bastard he was, with a healthy dose of selfishness thrown in for good measure.

Until this moment, he hadn't realized how much he'd been looking forward to hanging out with Burke and doing what bachelors did. Commitment changed everything and for Burke's sake, he hoped it was for the better. For Sloan's sake, it wasn't, but he couldn't help thinking about his luscious landlady and the until-death-do-us-part vow she'd made to the man she'd loved and lost. Had it been worth the price she'd paid and was still paying?

That thought made him more curious than he wanted to be about Maggie Potter.

In her office above the Harvest Café, Maggie stared at the spreadsheet displayed on her computer monitor. A few minutes ago the numbers had all looked good, but now she couldn't tell. Her eyes were starting to cross and everything blurred together.

When her vision cleared, she glanced at her watch and couldn't believe it was already two-thirty in the afternoon. On top of that, she hadn't eaten lunch. Downstairs the noon rush was probably over, making this a good time to grab some food.

She took the stairway right outside her office and walked down to the first floor, entering the café through a back entrance into the kitchen. The bowls, plates and utensils in the stainless-steel sink and on food preparation areas showed signs of exactly how rushed the rush had been, and it was good news for their bottom line. Her partner was standing in the doorway between front and back, keeping an eye out for customers.

"My head is about to explode," Maggie said. "Any chance of getting something to eat?"

Lucy Bishop smiled the smile that could have put her on magazine covers in swimsuits if her career path had taken her in that direction. Fortunately for Maggie, her friend was more interested in business than bikinis. She was a gorgeous, blue-eyed strawberry blonde who was forever being underestimated by men. It was immensely entertaining to watch them swallow their tongues and lose brain function in her presence.

"How about one of my world-famous chicken wraps with the secret sauce?"

"I don't expect you to wait on me. You've been busy, too. I'll make something myself."

"Keep protesting," Lucy said. "By the time you run out of steam I'll have your order up."

Maggie heard the words but they didn't register. Her attention was focused on the sidewalk outside the café and the man who'd just parked his Range Rover in a space out front.

Sloan Holden.

The problem with taking a break from hard work was that there wasn't anything to distract you from things you'd been deliberately not thinking about. Like seeing this big, strong man being gentle and protective with her daughter that morning. She couldn't reconcile that man with the one who was a global heartbreaker.

The real question was why she didn't want to think about him, and the best answer she could come up with was that he unsettled her.

"Maggie?"

"Hmm?" She looked at Lucy. "I'm sorry. What did you say?"

"I'm making you a wrap." Her partner automatically looked over when the door opened and Sloan walked in. She made a purring sound and said, "Right after I have that man's baby. Holy Toledo, he's a fifteen on a scale of one to ten."

"And he's my newest boarder."

"Sloan Holden?" Lucy lowered her voice but turned her back on the newcomer just to make sure he didn't hear.

"That's him," she confirmed.

"You have to introduce me."

"Of course," Maggie said, then the two of them walked over to where he stood by the sign that politely asked customers to wait to be seated. "Hi."

"Maggie." His gaze slid to her partner. "I've heard nothing but good things about the food here and decided to see for myself if the rumors are true."

"They're true," Maggie confirmed. "And that is all due to the culinary skills of my business partner. Sloan Holden, this is Lucy Bishop."

"Nice to meet you." He held out his hand.

Lucy shook it. "The pleasure is all mine. Isn't it a little late for lunch? Or is this an early dinner?"

"Lunch. I lost track of time."

"I always say it takes a special kind of stupid to for-get to eat."

Maggie watched Lucy give him the smile that had made many a man putty in her hands, but Sloan didn't bat an eye.

"Then, label me a moron because that's the best excuse I can come up with," he said.

"You're in good company." Lucy met her gaze. "Maggie just surfaced, too, and realized she hadn't eaten."

"Then, you should keep me company. I hate to eat alone," he said. "And we dim-witted workaholics should stick together."

"Thanks," she said, "but I'm just going to take some-thing back to my desk."

"I don't recommend that." He raised an eyebrow. "A break from work is food for the soul. That's just as impor-tant as nutrition for the body."

There was no graceful way out of this, so she was better off just sucking it up. "You're right. Let's sit over there."

The place was empty of customers at the moment and Maggie pointed to a table in a far corner that wasn't visible through the front window. She grabbed a couple of menus and followed him. He was wearing dark slacks and a pale yellow dress shirt, different from the one her daughter had streaked banana on early this morning.

She was very proud of the way the café had turned out. The interior was decorated in fall colors—orange, gold, green and brown. The walls had country touches: an old washboard, shelves with metal pitchers and pictures of fruit and vegetables. It was cozy and comfortable. But probably light-years from the places Sloan went to.

They sat at a small round table covered by a leaf-print tablecloth. Two sets of utensils wrapped in ginger-colored napkins rested on either side.

After looking over the choices, he met her gaze. "What do you recommend?"

"Everything." She smiled. "Obviously I'm prejudiced, but even the vegetarian selections are yummy. But my favorite is the chicken wrap. Lucy makes a dressing that is truly unbelievably good."

"Sold," he said.

When Lucy came over, they both ordered it and she promised to bring them out in a few minutes.

Maggie was watching Sloan's face when Lucy walked away and saw the barest flicker of male appreciation. She felt a flicker of something herself and wasn't sure what to call it. Envy? A visceral response? Whatever the label, she didn't especially like the feeling and wanted to counteract it.

"She's really pretty, isn't she?"

Sloan met her gaze. "Yes, she is."

"This small town is probably very different from what you're used to." Maggie knew that for a fact just from reading tabloid stories about him. "It can be lonely."

"There's lots of work to keep me busy."

"I heard somewhere that breaks from work are food for the soul as important as nutrition for the body."

His expression was wry. "Remind me to be careful what I say to you."

"My point is—and I do have one—you should ask Lucy out," she said.

"Oh?" There was curiosity in his expression, but he also looked amused.

"Yes. She's beautiful and smart. Not to mention an awesome cook."

"Until our food arrives, I'll have to take your word on her culinary ability. And we barely spoke, so it was hard to tell whether or not she's smart. But she is very pretty."

"So ask her out." The little bit Lucy had said was a big clue that she wouldn't say no. Maggie unrolled the silverware from her napkin and set it on the table.

"Why should I?" he asked.

"She's single. And so are you." She settled the cloth napkin in her lap. "Unless you're dating someone."

"I'm not." He met her gaze. "But it's a well-documented fact that I'm a confirmed bachelor."

"I have read that you have a reputation for quantity over commitment. But Lucy isn't looking for Mr. Right."

"Any particular reason?"

Yes, but Maggie had no intention of saying anything about that to Sloan, mostly because she didn't know why. Instead, she countered, "Any particular reason you won't commit?"

For the first time since he'd walked into the café the amiable and amused expression on his face cracked slightly. She'd struck a nerve, and that was annoying because she hadn't thought he had any.

"Why does any man resist committing?" he said, not really answering.

"Good question. Color me curious. And all the more determined to convince you to ask Lucy out on a date."

"For the life of me, I can't figure out what your stake is in my personal life."

"That's because you don't understand the fundamental dynamics of female friendship."

"Enlighten me."

"Communication and sharing," she said. "I'm curious about the man behind the tabloid headlines. Lucy could find out so much if you'd take her out to dinner. And she would tell me everything."

"Since you're the inquiring mind who wants to know,

why don't I cut out the middleman—or woman—and just take you out to dinner."

"Really?" She stared at him. "A widow with a small child?"

"Neither of those things means you can't go out with me. You may have heard. There are these handy-dandy people called babysitters."

That would only address the problem of what to do with Danielle when Maggie went out. She would still be a widow. But she had one irrefutable argument left.

"Look, Sloan, we both know I'm not the type of woman you go out with. In fact, just the opposite. I'm a business-woman and mother."

"True." His eyes narrowed on her. "But what if this is a conscious choice on my part to date a woman who is the polar opposite of my usual type? And I've simply used the tabloids and their stories to throw everyone off my real purpose? A deflection."

"You don't mean you're actually interested in some-one like me?"

"Don't I?"

Maggie had thought she had the upper hand in this ver-bal give-and-take. That she had him on the run. But his response stopped her cold. Of course, he was teasing. He had to be.

"Like I said—quantity over commitment. When would you have the time to troll for an ordinary woman?"

"You'd be surprised."

"We're talking about you," she said. "Nothing would surprise me."

"I'll take that as a challenge, Maggie Potter."

"If you're planning a campaign just to surprise me, I'd have to say that you have way too much time on your hands."

"Would it surprise you to know that I would really just like to get to know you?"

"Now you're simply trying to get a rise out of me. It's not going to work."

"We'll just have to wait and see." He studied her, and the intensity was disconcerting. "But I sense you pushing me away and can't help wondering about it. You don't go out, do you? Why is that? Why do you keep to yourself? Is there a reason you won't let yourself be happy?"

"I have priorities," she said. "And how do you know I don't go out? I'm perfectly capable of being happy. In fact, I am very happy."

And defensive, she realized. Pride went before a fall and it was a long way down when she'd thought she had him right where she wanted him.

Note to self, she thought. *Never underestimate this man.*

Chapter Three

"I love my daughter more than life itself, but I feel crushing shame for leaving her with my mom and enjoying myself with you guys."

Maggie was sitting at a bistro table in Bar None, Blackwater Lake's local drinking establishment, with her friends April Kennedy and Delanie Carlson. The latter had inherited the place from her dad, who had died the previous year.

"What you're experiencing is a curious phenomenon. It even has a name. Mom guilt," Delanie said.

She was another woman who made men turn into mindless idiots just by walking into a room. A blue-eyed redhead, she had just the right curves to fill out a pair of jeans. It was a weeknight and traditionally slow at Bar None, which made it ideal for their weekly evening out.

"I remember my mom saying the same thing." April tossed a strand of sun-streaked brown hair over her shoulder as a bittersweet expression slid into her hazel eyes. "She couldn't wait to get time to herself, but when it happened she missed me like crazy. I still miss her a lot."

"So it is a mom thing." Maggie took a sip of chardonnay, then looked at April, who had lost her mother to breast cancer. "And what you just said gives me hope and inspiration."

"How?"

"You were raised by a single mom. No dad in the picture. And you turned out okay. A successful businesswoman with your photography shop on Main Street."

"If I say I think my mother did a great job with me, does that sound conceited?"

"Of course not," Delanie answered. "It's just the truth."

Maggie looked forward to this night out with her friends. She'd cooked dinner for her boarders and Josie had agreed to get it on the table for Sloan. Whenever he was around, Maggie was jittery and nervous, so it was a relief to have an evening off.

"And what about you, Dee?" she asked. "How are you doing since your dad passed away? I know you two were close."

"I miss him." Delanie looked around the place she now owned.

The interior reflected the Montana pioneer spirit—rugged and rustic. Overhead, dark beams ran the length of the ceiling and the still-original floor was fashioned from wood planks. Lantern-shaped lights illuminated the booths lining the exterior and bistro tables scattered throughout. A rectangular oak bar with a brass foot rail dominated the center of the room, and pictures of the earliest Blackwater Lake settlers with shovels, axes and covered wagons hung on the walls.

Delanie glanced at her friends. "This may sound corny, but I can feel him here. Sort of a presence. It's comforting."

"That's good." Maggie envied her friend. She'd never experienced comfort or felt Danny's presence in the house he'd built for her. And when she looked at the daughter they'd made, sometimes she felt a guilt that had nothing to do with being a good mom and everything to do with a wife who'd let her husband down. He'd never had a chance to see his child.

"Okay, ladies," Dee said. "This conversation has taken a dark and twisty turn. I took the night off and am paying Savannah to pour drinks so that I can have a distraction from work."

April laughed. "Then, we picked the wrong place to distract you."

"There aren't a lot of places to go in a town this small," Maggie commented.

"That's going to change when the resort is built. Mark my words." April nodded knowingly. "Maybe you can convince your new boarder the builder to put up a movie theater."

"Or a shopping mall." Delanie's blue eyes took on a dreamy look. "I would happily indulge my love affair with shoes, especially the ones I didn't have to drive an hour to buy."

The other two thought about that and sighed dreamily.

"So what's he like?" Delanie asked. "I saw Lucy the other day and she said Sloan Holden came into the café and had lunch with you."

"What did Lucy say about him?" Maggie hedged.

"That he's charming and handsome."

Maggie's heart started beating just a little too fast as soon as his name came up. For the past couple of days she'd seen him at breakfast and dinner. And that one day for lunch. He was unfailingly polite, undemanding, and her daughter followed him around whenever she saw him. But what distracted Maggie most was what he'd said at lunch, the hint that he'd used serial dating as a cover until he found someone like her.

Surely he'd been teasing. Although, if he really was anticommitment, hooking up with a widow who wasn't interested in a relationship would certainly preserve his confirmed-bachelor status.

"So, is he?" April demanded.

Maggie blinked at her friends. "What?"

"Pay attention, Potter," Dee scolded. "Is he charming and handsome?"

"Oh, I'm not the best person to ask."

"Come on," April said. "You're a woman and you're breathing. We've watched movies together and rated the actors on a scale. If you can do that, you can give us an opinion."

"Since he's a paying customer, it seems unprofessional to talk about him like this."

Delanie frowned at her. "What's up? It isn't like you not to share."

"I'm uncomfortable with the one-to-ten thing."

"Okay. We'll compare him to actors and see how he holds up. I'll start." April took a sip of her wine. "Channing Tatum."

"Ooh," Maggie said. "But no. Sloan is in good shape, but more like a runner than a wrestler."

"Okay. How about Taylor Kitsch?" Delanie shrugged. "I just rented the movie *Battleship*. It was cheesy, but I loved it."

Maggie knew the actor and thought for a moment, then shook her head. "He and Chris Pratt are a similar type and both are fantasy-worthy, but I wouldn't say Sloan resembles them."

"Definitely fantasy material," April agreed. "I just saw the musical *Into the Woods* and I have to say that Chris Pine works for me in a big way as Prince Charming."

"Bingo," Maggie said. "He reminds me of Chris Pine, but with brown eyes and darker hair."

Delanie used her hand to fan herself. "Be still, my heart. And he's under your roof. How do you sleep at night?"

"Oh, you know. Exhausted after work, cooking for boarders and chasing after a toddler. I just close my eyes and…" *Think about being alone in my big bed while Sloan is alone in his on the second floor of my house.* "I'm sure you'll both get a chance to meet him. This is a small town and—"

The bell over the bar's front door tinkled and all three women looked over to see who'd walked in. Maggie instantly recognized Sloan, who smiled when he saw her.

"That's him," she whispered to her friends. "Sloan Holden."

Without hesitation, he walked over to their table. "Hi, Maggie. Mind if I join you ladies?"

Before Maggie could think of a way to discourage him, her two friends enthusiastically invited him to pull up a chair. He did and settled in right next to her.

"So you're Sloan Holden," Delanie said.

"Yes." He shook hands with her and April as they introduced themselves.

"What are you doing here?" Maggie asked. Then she realized that sounded just the tiniest bit abrupt and unwelcoming. "I mean, did you have dinner? Josie promised to put everything on the table for me. Since my mom has Danielle, it's a chance for me to have a night off."

"Yes, I did have dinner. Excellent pot roast, by the way. Josie mentioned that you were here and I felt like taking a night off myself."

The implication was that he'd come looking for her. Whether or not that was the case, the idea of it kicked up her pulse.

"Delanie owns Bar None," Maggie said.

He looked at the redhead. "I'm impressed. This is a nice place."

"Thanks. Would you like a drink?"

"Beer," he said. "Whatever you have on draft."

"Coming right up." Delanie slid off her chair and headed over to the bar, where the fill-in bartender was polishing glasses. She said something and the young woman grabbed a tall glass and filled it.

"April owns a photography studio," Maggie said, filling the silence.

"I've seen it." Sloan looked at the pretty brunette but gave no indication he noticed how pretty she was. "How's business?"

"A little slow when it's not ski or boating season. Tourism drops off then, but I diversify. Besides portraits and wedding pictures, I sell my photographs of landscapes and wildlife. I freelance for high school events and sometimes the sheriff's office needs photos taken."

"Sounds like you keep busy."

Delanie returned and set a glass on a napkin in front of him. "Welcome to Bar None. First one is on the house."

"Thank you."

For several moments, the four of them sipped their drinks in silence. Maggie could tell her friends felt a little uncomfortable after talking about him. Then he'd walked in and it was a little like getting caught with their hands in the cookie jar. She was preoccupied because his thigh kept brushing hers. He seemed bigger at this bistro table than he did in her dining room. She needed to act normal because her friends would notice, but she didn't feel at all normal around Sloan.

"So, Mr. Holden—"

"Sloan, please," he said.

"Sloan," April finally said. "I have a confession to make."

"Yeah. We need to come clean," Delanie chimed in, obviously aware of what her friend was going to say. "We were talking about you when you came in. Gossiping, really."

"Oh?" Sloan didn't look the least bit upset.

April nodded. "For the record, Maggie protected the privacy of her guest and wouldn't cooperate. The thing is, this is a small town and not much happens. People gossip anyway. But when we have a celebrity, there's going to be talk. And Bar None is gossip central, so we were doing our duty as loyal customers and citizens of Blackwater Lake."

"I see your point." Sloan held up his beer mug, signaling a toast. "To loyalty."

They all clinked glasses and sipped.

"What do you want to know about me?" Sloan asked.

"So many things, so little time." Delanie grinned. "Okay, since you volunteered... Why are you a confirmed bachelor?"

"Because I was married for fifteen minutes and found out I'm not good at it." The answer was straightforward, matter-of-fact. No tension or evidence he'd been deeply hurt.

And then his muscular thigh bumped against Maggie's and her nerves snapped, crackled and popped. Her gaze jumped to his and she saw laughter in his eyes. The table was small, but she would bet that he was deliberately touching her.

"What if you fall in love?" April wanted to know.

"I don't believe in it. Simple, uncomplicated and fun. That's all I'm looking for."

"You're honest. That's pretty cute." Delanie looked impressed. "But I think you should have that sentiment stitched on a sampler and mounted on the wall of your office."

"Great idea. I'll get my assistant right on that."

"Not if you want her to continue being your assistant," Maggie said.

"You're probably right. Next question."

"Can we talk you into building a movie theater in Blackwater Lake? Maybe a multiplex?"

"Why?"

"Someplace to go if we had a date," Delanie said.

"If?" He looked at each of them in turn, but his gaze settled on Maggie. "Now that I think about it, why are three beautiful ladies such as yourselves not on a date right now?"

"Who says we want to date?" Maggie answered, thinking about what he'd said to her, about her not wanting to be happy. "We are successful businesswomen—fulfilled and content without a man."

"Is it just me," he said to April and Delanie, "or does she sound defensive?"

Why was he going there? Maggie thought. The last time they'd talked, he'd agreed that she wasn't his type. So why was he zeroing in on her? She didn't for a second buy his story about using tabloid interviews referencing him being a confirmed bachelor as a cover to look for someone like her. And then it dawned on her that he was flirting. It took a while to recognize the behavior because no one had flirted with her in a very long time.

"Not defensive." She smiled at him and crossed one leg over the other. The movement brought their thighs into contact and she saw his eyes darken for a second. "Just telling it like it is."

"So that's what you say to all the guys?"

"No," she said. "Just the ones who sell newspapers because of their escapades with women."

The zinger made him grin and she felt that look all the

way to her toes. She smiled back at him and realized she'd forgotten how much fun flirting could be.

When Sloan got back to the house after leaving the bar, he poured himself a scotch from the bottle his assistant had requested for his room and took the tumbler outside. It was a beautiful March night—cool, crisp, clear. He didn't think he'd ever seen a more spectacular sky full of stars.

A little while ago he'd heard Maggie come home with Danielle. The open master-bedroom window backed up to the patio where he was sitting and the sounds of giggling and splashing drifted to him. It was bath time and all indications pointed to the fact that the girls were having a blast.

For some reason it made him feel lonely, again on the outside looking in. Especially after hanging out with Maggie at Bar None. She'd actually flirted with him and rubbed her leg against his, mostly, he suspected, because she was aware that he'd been deliberately doing that to her. He grinned at the memory even as his body grew hard with need. The attraction was unexpected and inconvenient, and he should have known better than to start something he had no intention of finishing. He'd been playing with fire and the burning inside him now was his punishment.

The voices inside the house became more subdued and then the light went off. Moonlight was now the only light source in the rear yard. He was almost sure Maggie was singing to her daughter, and then all was quiet. Moments later, he heard the microwave go on in the kitchen. The outside door opened and Maggie stepped onto the patio.

Sloan was pretty sure she didn't see him, because she stood still, looking at the sky and taking deep, cleansing breaths. He figured it would be best to warn her she wasn't alone.

"Maggie—"

"Dear God—" She jumped and let out a screech, pressing a hand to her chest. "You scared me."

"Sorry."

"I thought you'd be upstairs."

"No. I wanted some air," he explained.

"Me, too." She blew out a long breath then met his gaze.

She was close enough that he could reach out and touch her. He really wanted to, which meant it probably wasn't a very good idea.

"It's a beautiful night," he said.

"I don't want to intrude. And I didn't have dinner. I just put a plate in the microwave. You were here first."

"Is there anything in the Potter House rules that says we can't enjoy the fresh air together?"

"Of course not." Moonlight revealed her mouth curving up in a smile.

"Danielle is settled for the night?"

"She is."

"Then, you should take some time to enjoy the beauty of your own backyard." He saw her catch her bottom lip between her teeth and need sliced through him, sharp and deep. "I'll bet you don't do it very much."

"You'd win that bet."

"Take a chance, Potter. Throw caution to the wind. Five minutes to fill up your soul."

She sighed and he knew he'd won this round. There was a thickly padded chair at a right angle to his and she lowered herself into it.

"No guilt allowed." In front of him her friends had teased her about feeling guilty for enjoying an evening away from her daughter. "Whatever you have to do inside will still be there when your spirit is renewed."

"That's for sure," she agreed. "Somehow the B and B

fairies never make it here to get breakfast ready or do laundry."

"It's just sad. You can't get good fairy help these days."

She laughed. "You're very funny, Sloan."

"I'm glad you think so."

"April and Delanie thought so, too." She met his gaze. "They told me after you left."

"So that's why my ears were burning."

"Oh, please. A man who spends as much time as you do with a vast number of women couldn't possibly be surprised that we talked about you after you left."

"I'm not at all surprised. Especially since your friends came right out and copped to the fact that you were discussing me before I got there."

"You gotta love honest gossipmongers," she pointed out.

"It was refreshing. And I liked your friends very much."

"As I said, the feeling is mutual. You were exceptionally charming tonight, Holden."

"I did my best."

"Do you remember when you said we could ask you anything?"

"Yes."

"Well, you may also recall that I never asked a question at all."

He did. "I'm sensing that you would like to now. Am I right?"

"Yes. And I have several, if that's okay."

"Should I be afraid?"

"I promise it won't hurt," she said.

"Okay, then." He set his empty tumbler on the outside coffee table. "What would you like to know?"

"Did you follow me to Bar None tonight?"

"That makes me sound like a stalker," he hedged.

"Are you?"

"Wow. I'm not sure if going from serial killer to stalker is a step up."

She folded her arms over her chest. "You're very good at not answering questions."

"Lots of practice," he admitted. "Okay. It's a hard habit to break, but I'll stop sidestepping. When Josie mentioned that you were meeting friends it sounded like fun and I did deliberately crash the party."

He couldn't speak to how hard it was being a single mom and needing some downtime. But he knew how it felt to be a fish out of water, a big fish in a little pond and craving some social time. Not to mention being curious about Maggie. He braced himself for a grilling about following her.

"Why would you do that?"

"I needed to talk to someone about something other than work."

"Oh." She nodded. "I understand that. And then my friends asked you to build a movie theater."

"It's actually a great idea. The resort is going to bring in a lot of people. They'll be looking for entertainment involving something other than skiing or boating and water sports."

"Speaking of entertainment…" She tapped her lip. "Is it true that a woman once broke into your hotel room and waited in your bed? Naked?"

He groaned. "Don't remind me."

"So it is true." She leaned forward, warming to her subject. "You make it sound like a bad thing."

"By definition, breaking into my hotel room *is* bad."

"Surely not the naked part." Her tone was teasing.

"Whose side are you on? I was the injured party."

"You sound like an outraged spinster. I don't understand your problem. Was she fat? Cellulite? Abs weren't prime-time ready?"

"She had a lovely body. Hotel security thought so, too, as did the police. Why would this be okay because I'm a guy? She violated my personal space."

"I see what you mean." She scooted to the edge of her chair. "There was another story about you spending millions of dollars on breakup baubles."

"Baubles?" That's one he hadn't heard. Apparently he wasn't aware of all his publicity.

"Yes. Diamond tennis bracelets. Emerald pendants. Sapphire earrings. If this is true, it could explain why women throw themselves at you. Naked," she added.

"For the tasteful parting gift?"

"Yes. That's a heck of a consolation prize."

"Well, it's not true." The only woman who'd received a significant parting gift was his wife when he divorced her for cheating on him. Getting rid of her had been worth every penny it had cost him. He didn't care so much for himself. The mistake had been his, as were the consequences. But she'd hurt his family and he'd paid the price of protecting them. And he would do it again if necessary.

"There was another story that got a lot of attention. Something about you not being very good in bed. And a very bad kisser."

"Your friends didn't ask this many questions," he pointed out.

"Maybe their minds aren't as inquiring as mine. In all fairness, less-than-satisfied lady was one of the women scorned and the story had all the signs of being about revenge."

He stood. "How do you remember this stuff?"

"It's fascinating." She stood up, too.

"Well, I feel like an exhibit at the zoo." He was an inch

away from her, close enough to feel the warmth of her body and smell the sweet scent of her skin. "I think I hear the microwave signaling your plate of food is warm."

"So was it about revenge? Or are you lacking in the romance department?"

"Is there any way to make you stop this interrogation?"

"Feed me." She met his gaze and there was a sassy expression on her face. "Or kiss me."

It wasn't often that someone surprised Sloan, but Maggie did now. He remembered her saying this wouldn't hurt a bit, but now he wasn't so sure. The question was whether or not it would hurt more if he *didn't* kiss her. Hell and damnation, this was a dilemma. But he didn't get where he was in the business world by not taking a risk.

He curved his fingers around her upper arms and pulled her close, his gaze intent on her mouth. "I'll take door number two."

Chapter Four

Maggie had no idea why she'd dared Sloan to feed or kiss her, but when his lips touched hers she was really glad he'd picked the second option. His mouth was soft, gentle, tentative and tempting all at the same time. Her heart was racing and her knees were weak, but he was holding her and she trusted him not to let her go.

He whispered against her mouth, "Any more questions?"

"Hmm?" The only question on her mind was why he wasn't still kissing her. "I can't think of any."

"Okay, then." He slid his arms around her and pulled her close, then kissed her again.

It felt so good to be held and touched, wrapped in a pair of strong arms and pressed against a man's body. She was pretty sure her toes were actually curling, and it was the most wonderful thing that had happened to her for longer than she could remember.

Time seemed to stop and she wanted to stay suspended in this sensuous dimension. Right here, right now, while she kissed Sloan Holden on her patio under the stars, there was no guilt, worry or doubt about being a single mom. She was simply a woman enjoying everything about being female and savoring this bold man who wasn't afraid of a challenge. Sloan slid his fingers into her hair, cupping her head to make the pressure of their mouths more firm. His breathing was unsteady and it was thrilling to know she'd affected him, too.

And then she heard Danielle cry out. The sound came through the open window and reality rushed back like a slap in the face. She was a mother first and foremost. Maggie froze, waiting, and the sound came again, pouring in along with guilt, worry and even more doubt about her ability to do a decent job of raising her child alone. Look how easily this man had distracted her.

She took two steps back, away from the warmth of his body, and hating herself for missing it. "I need to check on my daughter."

"Right. Of course." He dragged his fingers through his hair. "Do I need to apologize for that?"

"Is that what your gut is telling you to do?"

He shook his head. "But the look on your face right now is making me think it might be a good idea."

What he was seeing on her face probably had more to do with astonishment. She had believed the part of her that could be turned on had died with her husband. But she was so wrong. Sloan had stirred something up and she wanted to settle it back down again.

"There's nothing to be sorry for. It was my fault." She played with her fingers, twisting them together nervously. "I have to go to Danielle."

And begin the process of forgetting about this kiss.

Several days went by and Maggie realized she was looking at time passing and putting it in two columns: before and after that kiss. She saw Sloan at breakfast and dinner, doing her best to go back to being his hospitable, professional but friendly landlady and not the woman who'd challenged him to kiss her. She talked to him as little as

possible and he didn't push the issue by striking up a conversation. And there was a conclusion to be drawn from
that. He regretted the kiss, too.

She set a platter of scrambled eggs and hash browns on
the dining room table, where Sloan and Josie were sitting.
The fruit and freshly baked muffins were already there.

"Can I freshen anyone's coffee?" she asked.

"I'm good." Sloan barely glanced up from the newspaper he was reading.

"Me, too." Josie was giving her a quizzical look.

"All right, then. Let me know if you need anything."
She left the room.

Her daughter sat in the high chair eating half a banana.
If she hadn't been, she would have been bugging Sloan. As
if Maggie needed another one, that was a good reason to
back off from him. And that was what she'd been doing,
pretty successfully, in her opinion.

A half hour later, Sloan said goodbye and headed for
the door. Danielle called out, "Bye-bye," and wiggled her
fingers in her version of a wave. That earned the little girl
a big grin from Sloan, but Maggie was the one who felt the
power of it. And a pang of disappointment that he hadn't
aimed the warmth at her.

Josie brought plates and platters into the kitchen. "Are
you going to tell me what's going on?"

"I'd be happy to if you'd be more specific."

The other woman started rinsing off plates and putting
them in the dishwasher. "I'm talking about you and Sloan.
Since he arrived, there's been a nice friendly vibe going on
between the two of you. And in the past couple days it's
changed. You barely speak, and it can only be described
as awkward. What the heck happened?"

That kiss happened, Maggie thought. She'd gone over it
a thousand times. He never would have done it if she hadn't

put the suggestion out there. Over and over she wondered why she had. Maybe the glass of wine. Possibly it was all the flirty talk and leg touching while sitting beside him at Bar None. The lingering effects of that might have made those fateful words come out of her mouth. Oh, how she wanted them back.

Josie was a friend as well as one of her boarders. But Maggie was proceeding on the hope that not talking about what happened on the patio would make it go away.

"You think we're acting awkward?"

"And how." Standing by the sink, Josie put a hand on her hip. "And don't think I didn't notice that you just answered a question with a question and gave no information at all."

Maggie was kind of hoping that one had slipped by, but no such luck. "Would I do that?"

"Seriously, Maggie? You just did it again. That only confirms my suspicion that there's something going on with the two of you."

"Knock, knock." The front door opened and in walked Maggie's mom, Maureen O'Keefe. She had brown eyes and dark hair shot through with silver, cut in a piecey style with the back flipped up. She smiled at Danielle, then walked over and cupped her granddaughter's small face in both hands before kissing her forehead. "Hello, my precious little girl."

"Hi, Mom." Maggie was grateful for the distraction. "Once upon a time I was your precious girl."

"You still are." Her mom walked over and cupped her face in her hands, then kissed her forehead. "Hi, Josie. Are we still on for shopping?"

"Just as soon as your precious girl—the grown-up one—comes clean about what's going on between her and the new guy."

Maureen's brown eyes turned wary. "There's something

going on? Between you and Sloan Holden? I'm going to have to meet him."

"Oh, please—" Maggie tried to look as innocent as possible.

"See?" Josie pointed at her. "That's the kind of answer I've been getting. Which is to say no answer at all. You're her mother. Surely you can get her to talk."

"Can you give me a little context?" Maureen said.

"I can see where that would help." Josie thought for a moment. "Like I just said to Maggie—since he got here things have been friendly and fun. Easy. That changed a couple of days ago and you'd think we're having another ice age the way these two act. Makes me want to put on a parka every time they're in the same room."

The two older women stared at her expectantly and Maggie squirmed. She felt like a kid caught doing something wrong when her only motive was to try to do the right thing. "It's all about being a professional. Creating a comfortable, uncomplicated space for my guests. I've never run a bed-and-breakfast before, so I'm experimenting with just the right feeling and mood."

Maggie saw a look on her mom's face and not for the first time wished the woman couldn't see through her like a piece of clear plastic.

"Really?" Maureen said skeptically. "I know you, Margaret Mary Potter."

Uh-oh. It was never good when her mom used all three names. Made her want to walk herself into a corner and face the wall until she was told her time-out was over. "Yes, you do."

"Josie's right. Something is up and you're avoiding it like the black death. What did that man do to you?"

Well, this was a fine mess. She wanted to bury her head in the sand and ignore what had happened. But she couldn't let them believe Sloan had harmed her. He'd shaken her up, but there was no permanent damage done. She would get back her perspective and all would be well. As long as these two women got an answer to their questions.

"It was nothing, really."

"Then, you won't mind sharing details," her mom said. "What was it, *really*?"

"He kissed me." Maggie shrugged.

"Well, then," Josie said, her tone full of approval. "When?"

"Where?" Maureen asked. "Here? In the bedroom?"

"That's not important," Maggie protested.

"It kind of is," her boarder said. "You know the only way this inquisition stops is when we get all the facts."

"That's not happening. And if you guys insist on pushing the issue, you're going to miss out on the early-bird specials at the mall."

"Come on, Maggie. I'm your mother. Put yourself in my shoes. What if Danielle wouldn't tell you about something going on in her life?"

Maggie nearly knuckled. Her mom was really good at applying just the right amount of motivational guilt. But she held back.

"You are my mother and I love you." She unstrapped Danielle from the high chair and lifted her out to toddle around the room. "But there really is nothing more than that to tell. He kissed me and we both realized it meant nothing."

"Not from the ice age I've been living in," Josie muttered. "Don't be too hasty about this."

"It's not a rush to judgment. It's reality. I'm a widow with a daughter to raise. He was in *People* magazine's 'most eligible millionaire bachelor' issue. If that doesn't make us incompatible enough, he has a playboy reputation. Love 'em and leave 'em."

"But he's so sweet with Danielle. Maybe he just hasn't met the right woman yet," Josie suggested.

"He's met dozens of women, and if none of them were right it's because he's not interested in making a commitment." Maggie looked at both women and sighed. "He's a nice man. And he seems good with children. But a good deal of evidence points to the fact that he's all flirt and no depth."

"Are you sure you're not just projecting that on him? Stereotyping him so he's not a threat?" her mom asked.

"I'm not labeling him that way. Magazines and newspapers have reported on his activities. It's all flash and no substance. A game. I'm too busy for games. So it's best if we avoid each other."

"But—"

"No, Mom. No buts. I'm a mother and a businesswoman. There's no room in my life for a man. Especially one like Sloan Holden."

She grabbed up her daughter and whisked her into the other room for a diaper change before the two older women could gang up on her again. It was for the best that she steer clear of Sloan, and thank goodness he was avoiding her, too.

Nearly a week after Sloan had kissed Maggie, he was pretty sure he was losing his mind. Up until that complete and utter failure of judgment when he'd touched his mouth to hers and found out she tasted even more amazing than he'd imagined, his business focus had been notorious, in a good way. His cousin had said more than once that he was like a computer, all circuits firing, efficiency central.

It had all changed after that kiss under the stars.

In the past couple of days he'd forgotten meetings, and in the ones he'd attended, his mind had wandered to the spectacular way Maggie's backside filled out a pair of jeans when she bent over the oven to pull out a pan of blueberry muffins. Then first thing this morning, his assistant had asked him for the quarterly reports he'd brought home last night to look over. And he had looked them over. Corrections were all neatly marked and initialed. But it didn't do her any good because he'd left the B and B without his briefcase that morning.

He'd been in a hurry to get out of there before someone noticed he was staring at Maggie. Couldn't seem to keep himself from looking at her when there were more muffins and bending over. Yeah, he was going to hell.

But first he had to go back and retrieve the briefcase full of work that his assistant needed. It was midmorning and he figured Josie was volunteering as usual at the library and Maggie was at the café by now. The coast would be clear and he was in his car and nearly there.

He turned right off the main road and followed the narrow street to the end, where the log home that was Potter House stood. In the semicircular driveway he saw her dark blue SUV with the tailgate open and the cargo area filled with grocery bags. Maggie was leaning into the rear passenger seat, filling out those jeans almost as nicely as when she took something out of the oven.

So much for the coast being clear.

He groaned and wondered what he'd done to tick off fate and what he could do to turn around his bad luck. In his opinion, the best option was to pretend nothing had happened. Just the way Maggie was doing.

He opened his car door and got out, prepared to say hello and pretend, for all he was worth, that the kiss had been no big deal and everything was normal. That was when he heard the high-pitched wails coming from the rear seat of her car.

"Come on, Danielle. Mommy doesn't have time for this. I have to unload the groceries. Food is melting."

The quietly spoken, utterly reasonable words had no effect on the completely unreasonable toddler, and the screaming continued. Sloan wanted to retrieve his briefcase and go back to his office. None of this was his problem. But he couldn't do it.

"Hi, Maggie," he said, walking up to the open tailgate. "I'll get those bags."

She straightened and met his gaze, a puzzled expression on her face. "Aren't you supposed to be at work? What are you doing here?"

And wasn't that the million-dollar question. Telling the truth was best. He didn't have to get into all of it. "I left some paperwork here and my assistant needs it today."

"Then, you should get it to her." Maggie's voice got a little louder in order to be heard above the wailing coming from the backseat of her car. "I've got this."

Not from where he was standing. "I'm sure you do, but since I'm here, it will just take a couple of minutes to get the groceries into the house. I'll do that while you take care of Shorty."

The look of stubborn independence on her face said she was going to push back. While he admired her character, arguing was a waste of breath. He was stubborn, too, and in the time it would take for a conversation, he could have all the groceries in the kitchen.

Without a word, he reached into the cargo area of the SUV and took as many bags as he could carry.

"Hold on," she said, racing past him and up the stairs to the front door. "I'll unlock it."

"Thanks," he said, moving past her.

"No. Thank you." And then she went back to the car and liberated her daughter from the car seat.

Sloan passed her in the living room on his way out for a second trip. Maggie had her child in one arm and a bag in the other. She tried to put the little girl down, but the toddler pulled her legs up, refusing to stand. And she was crying her eyes out. At that rate, it would have taken her all day to unload the car. Maybe it was a good thing he'd lost his mind and forgotten work material.

In a few minutes everything had been transferred from her car to the kitchen. Sloan was about to go upstairs to get the paperwork he'd forgotten when he realized Maggie was only using one hand to put things away because her other arm was full of little girl. So the secret was out. That was how she maintained her fantastic figure. No expensive gym membership for her. Being a working mom was how she stayed in shape.

Danielle had stopped crying, but she was taking deep, shuddering breaths that would tug at the hardest heart. Sloan just couldn't leave her like this.

He walked over to where Maggie was working on the other side of the island. "I have no idea where any of this stuff goes, but maybe she'll let me hold her."

Maggie shook her head. "She's really cranky. A very bad night. I think she's teething. But we were almost out of everything. I had to take her with me."

Sloan wondered if Maggie wasn't used to accepting help or if there was a chip on her shoulder about proving to the world she could do it alone. Either way, he was here right now and wouldn't leave without at least trying to give her a hand.

"I can see that she's cranky and I'm not afraid."

"I can't ask you to do that, Sloan."

"You didn't." He held out his arms to the kid. "What do you say, Shorty? Want to give your mom a break?"

"I don't think she'll go for it."

"Maybe not." He kept his arms extended while the child thought it over. Finally, hesitantly, Danielle leaned toward him and he took her. "What do you know."

"Wow." Maggie looked surprised, then determined. "I'll hurry and get everything put away so we don't keep you very long."

"No rush."

"But you have to get back to work," she pointed out.

"A few minutes one way or the other won't make much difference." He walked around, and the toddler's slight weight felt surprisingly good in his arms. Her face was wet, but she sighed, and the deep, hiccuping breaths stopped. "Feeling better, kiddo?"

She rubbed a chubby fist beneath her runny nose then dragged it over the front of his shirt. A very expensive tissue, he thought. When she calmed down, he set her on the great-room floor beside the toy basket pushed beneath an end table. He rummaged through it, looking for the talking thing, the one with the button beside an animal. When it was pushed, a voice named the critter and made the correct creature sound. He'd seen Maggie do this with her.

He pushed the cow and Danielle immediately said, "Moo."

"Right. Good job." He pushed the frog.

"Bet," she said.

"Pretty close. Ribbet," he told her.

She pushed the lion and made a roaring sound, or the two-year-old version of it. He sat on the floor and she plopped herself into his lap and held the toy out to him. It didn't take a PhD in parenting to realize what she wanted.

Sloan touched the horse and said, "Horse."

She tried to repeat the word and did a pretty good job. Then, plain as day, she said, "Cookie."

"Even I understood that," he said to Maggie.

"Of course." She glanced over her shoulder after shoving a box of cereal into a cupboard. "And she's very accomplished at saying no, too."

"Cookie," the little girl said again.

"You'll spoil your lunch, baby girl," her mother said. "And they're messy."

"If it was up to me," he said to the child, "you could have a whole bag. Fortunately, your mother is not a pushover." He looked at Maggie. "What do you say? Maybe just one for putting that little meltdown behind her?"

"Is that all it takes?" She was shaking her head at the same time she smiled at him. "A few tears and a woman can have whatever she wants?"

"You know how it is. Men are completely helpless when a female cries." He met her teasing gaze. "And I'm not ashamed to admit it."

"Cookie," Danielle said impatiently.

"I was sort of hoping she'd forget," he admitted.

Maggie laughed. "You are an optimist, aren't you? When it comes to *c-o-o-k-i-e-s*—" she spelled the word "—my daughter has single-minded determination that is legendary."

"Okay." He looked at the little girl, who was staring back at him with an expression he interpreted as expecting him to go to battle for her. "It's up to your mom, kid."

"No, it's up to you," Maggie said. "If I give her one, that pretty white shirt of yours won't be so pretty and white anymore."

"Well—" he looked at the stain already streaking his chest "—she already used it to wipe her nose. A few crumbs can hardly do too much more damage."

"For the record, I'm sorry about your shirt and I will wash it." Maggie sighed. "But if you think it can't get much worse, you really are a rookie."

"No big deal on the shirt. My point is that I have to change it anyway. So I vote in favor of a *c-o-o-k-i-e*."

"Okay, then." She opened the brand-new bag of chocolate-chip cookies on the counter beside her, then reached in to grab one. Absently, she picked up the bag and walked over to him. She held up the treat and said to her daughter, "What's this, baby girl?"

"Cookie!" Happily she snatched it out of her mother's hand and shoved it in her mouth.

That made Sloan a little nervous. "Is she going to choke on that?"

"It scared me, too, the first time, but she'll be fine." She held out the bag to him. "Cookie?"

"Thanks." He reached in and took one.

There was an odd expression on Maggie's face. "Don't look now, but your playboy image is taking a direct hit. If they could see you eating cookies with a two-year-old, what would your women say?"

"It's not so much what they would say as what they might do," he said.

"No more scantily clad babes hiding in your room?"

"If that were the case, I'd put a picture on social media myself. But me with a child would ratchet up the marriage minded, and speculation would run rampant about the end of my eligible-bachelor days. Stalking would be off the chart."

"Really?" Maggie looked genuinely surprised.

"Yes. Do you have any idea how inconvenient and annoying it is to have a stranger show up in your bed uninvited?"

"So you want to personally invite your women into your bed?"

Sloan would personally invite Maggie there in a heartbeat, and the instantaneous thought sent a sliver of need straight through him. Clearly she was joking or he would have extended an invitation right then and there. Then Danielle wiped a grubby hand over his chest, leaving a trail of chocolate and crumbs. That brought him down to earth. Even if Maggie was willing to accept an invitation into his bed, there was no way anything could happen with this little one to take care of.

Oddly enough, that didn't bother him. And it wasn't his bachelor-playboy image he was concerned about. He realized how much he liked being a part of this scenario, entertaining a child and hanging out with her mother. It filled up a part of his soul that he'd put aside for a long time. Since his divorce, he'd consciously avoided personal complications. After a failed marriage, the last thing he wanted was to get serious about a woman who was still in love with the man she'd lost.

He needed work and lots of it to focus more completely on the resort project. No more thinking about kissing Maggie.

Or inviting her into his bed.

Chapter Five

Maggie thought she had put that kiss with Sloan into perspective and had her life back under control until he had come to the house unexpectedly a couple of days ago. It had been an awful morning with a fussy toddler, but she'd had business responsibilities. Things needed to be done, whether Danielle had wanted to come along or not. And she definitely had *not* wanted to.

After the grocery store, Maggie had had one nerve left from the nonstop crying all the way home. She'd never expected Sloan to come riding in like a white knight to the rescue, but white knight was a fitting description for a man who hauled in all those grocery bags in half the time it would have taken her. And she didn't think it was possible for him to be any sweeter to her daughter than he'd been that day. Watching the two of them was heartwarming, and at the same time it made her deeply sad that her husband had never had a chance to spend time with his daughter.

The problem wasn't Sloan; it was her. The threads of her life were delicately intertwined, but they fit together and were working. If one of those strings came loose and pulled free, it would all come apart. She was on an even keel and trying to stay that way. She didn't need a man coming in to unbalance her canoe, to mix a metaphor.

Her B and B was Sloan's temporary home and he had every right to come and go. So the lesson from his drop-in was to have her guard up at the house. In town she could probably avoid him. He was working, as was she, and the odds of their schedules intersecting were slim.

Still, she was vigilant on her way down Main Street from her office to the Grizzly Bear Diner, where she planned to meet her friend Jill Stone for lunch. Some would call it supporting her competition, but the two eating establishments provided very different dining experiences.

She walked into the diner and didn't see anyone at the podium displaying a sign that read, Please Wait to be Seated. The hostess must be busy somewhere else at the moment. Glancing into the area with booths and tables, she didn't see her friend, either. It would be hard to miss Jill's red hair, so obviously Maggie was the first to arrive.

She heard her cell phone ring and fished it out of her purse. "Hello."

"Maggie? It's Jill. I'm so sorry, but I can't make it. The school called just as I was on my way out the door to meet you. C.J. is sick and I have to pick him up."

C.J. was Jill's ten-year-old son. She also had a daughter about Danielle's age. Maggie knew how hard it was when a child was sick, and suspected it made no difference whether the child in question was two or ten.

"I'm so sorry to hear that," she said.

"I feel awful standing you up like this. But he's running a fever and has a sore throat. It came on suddenly, because he was fine when he went to school this morning."

"Don't worry about it, Jill. We'll put another date on the calendar when he's feeling better. I hope that's soon."

"Me, too," the worried mom said. "I might just drop in at the clinic and let Adam look him over."

Adam Stone was her husband, a family-practice doctor

at Mercy Medical Clinic here in town. He'd adopted the boy after marrying Jill. Come to think of it, her friend had been a single mom when the doctor had rented the apartment she owned that was upstairs from hers. The two had fallen in love, but any similarity between Jill's situation and Maggie's ended there.

C.J.'s dad had abandoned him and Danielle's father had died. If given the choice, Danny would have devoted himself to his child. Since he couldn't, Maggie would devote herself to the little girl enough for two parents.

"I think it's a good idea for C.J. to see a doctor," Maggie said. "If only to reassure you that there's nothing to worry about."

"It's very handy being married to a doctor," Jill said.

"I bet it is." Maggie laughed. "Don't let me keep you. Do me a favor. In a day or so give me a call and let me know how C.J. is doing."

"Will do. 'Bye, Maggie."

"Take care." Maggie pressed the stop button on her phone and turned to leave the diner. No point in staying. She would grab a sandwich at the café and eat it at her desk. Even though she'd been craving a burger and fries.

She reached out to push open the door, but it moved before she touched it. Sloan Holden walked in, backing her up several steps.

"This is a surprise," he said, smiling. "A nice one."

Her heart rate increased, just to let her know she thought it was nice, too. And ironic. Just minutes ago she'd been thinking that in town it would be much easier to avoid him. Not so much, apparently.

"I was just leaving," she said.

He looked at his watch. "Have you eaten already?"

"No. I was supposed to meet a friend, but she couldn't make it. Her son is sick."

"That's too bad."

They were standing a foot away from the hostess podium and a female voice said, "Two for lunch?"

Sloan hesitated just a moment before saying, "Yes."

Before Maggie could say they weren't together, he took her elbow and steered her after the hostess, who was leading the way. The next thing she knew, they were being seated at a secluded booth in the back.

"Brandon will be your server today. If there's anything I can get you, please don't hesitate to ask." She smiled at both of them. "Enjoy your lunch."

"Thanks." Sloan looked at her across the table. "This is unexpected, in a good way. I thought I was going to have to eat alone."

"You don't have to do this."

"What? Eat?" His mouth turned up at the corners. "Yeah, I kind of do."

"No. I meant you don't have to eat with me. Or keep me company. I'll just grab a sandwich and eat in my office."

"Oh, come on. You were planning to eat with someone. Why not me?"

So many reasons. "You might be planning to work." Since he wasn't carrying a briefcase or anything that looked remotely like work, it was a pretty weak excuse.

"I was planning to sit at the counter and chat up whoever was behind it. But a quiet booth with you is a lot more appealing." His dark brown eyes took on a pleading expression. "Come on. Do a lonely bachelor a favor. Be spontaneous. Have lunch with me."

"Lonely bachelor, my as-paragus," she teased. "If you're alone, it's only because this is Blackwater Lake and it's off the radar for your women."

"I'm going to ignore the 'my women' part of that statement and take the rest of it as affirmative that you'll join me for lunch."

"Okay. It's a yes. But only because I was looking forward to the Mama Bear burger combo."

"Good." He looked around, taking in the decor. Pictures of bears on the walls. Wallpaper with black paw prints on a cream background. The wild-animal ambience had everything but a stuffed grizzly in the corner. "This place has a lot of local color."

"That it does."

A nice-looking young man with brown hair and blue eyes who was in his late teens walked up with menus. "Hi. I'm Brandon and I'll be your server today."

Sloan held up a hand to stop him from leaving the menus. "I think we're ready to order."

"What can I get you?"

"I'll have a Mama Bear burger combo. Diet cola with lemon," Maggie said.

"Make mine a Papa Bear combo and coffee. Black."

"Coming right up," Brandon said.

Sloan watched the young man walk away and there were questions in his eyes. "Shouldn't he be in school?"

"He graduated from Blackwater Lake High School in June. He's taking some online classes while working to save money for college so he can go away in the fall."

"How do you know that?"

"His dad is a carpenter and works for McKnight Construction, not to be confused with McKnight Automotive where your cousin's fiancée works. Brandon's mom works at the grocery store and comes into the café. I hear things," she explained. "And it's a small town. So everyone hears things."

"I guess it's hard to keep a secret around here."

"Yes."

But no one knew Maggie's secret because she kept it to herself. No one knew Danny had wanted kids right after they'd married but Maggie had refused. She'd wanted to wait until his National Guard commitment was fulfilled. But she'd gotten pregnant and it hadn't been planned. That was the reason she had Danielle. And thank goodness she did. Best mistake ever. Or she would have nothing left of Danny.

"This town is very different from my stomping grounds."

"How?" She unwrapped eating utensils from the napkin and spread it in her lap. "Everything you do ends up in a newspaper, which means even more people know things."

"True. So tell me. Since there are no small-town tabloids, how does information spread in Blackwater Lake? Jungle drums?"

"Almost." She laughed. "But it works pretty much the way it does in the big city. Phone. Social media. Word of mouth."

His eyes darkened as it settled on *her* mouth. "Don't look now, but you're having a better time than you would have eating alone in your office."

"Says who? I really like my office and what I do."

"Me, too," he allowed. "But as I told you once before, everyone needs a break. Recharge your batteries. Let your hair down. Have a little fun."

"If you say so."

He studied her. "What do you have against having fun?"

"Nothing."

"That's not the impression I get," he said.

Although she had very little time for it, Maggie was completely open to having fun. As long as that fun didn't include a relationship. Maybe running into him was actually a sign. A good thing. They'd never talked about that kiss and probably should. Might be a good idea to clarify it, make sure he understood that she had boundaries.

"Believe me, Sloan, I like having fun as much as the next person. But..."

"What?" he asked when she hesitated.

"As long as it doesn't include kissing." Before he could say anything, she added, "I take full responsibility for what happened that night. What I said comes under the heading of not thinking it through."

"Your sense of accountability is extraordinarily acute. Last time I checked, it takes two to make a kiss." He met her gaze and there was amusement in his. "I believe I initiated that kiss and no one twisted my arm."

"All right. If you insist on splitting hairs, you can take half the blame. But you're flirting. Maybe you can't help yourself. It just comes naturally when you're around women. I need to be honest and straightforward. Just in case you're thinking about a repeat, I'm not going to kiss you again."

His eyebrows rose. "Really? You're absolutely certain about that?"

Maggie wasn't sure what kind of reaction she'd expected, but it probably included him looking more serious than amused. "Yes, really. I'm very serious about this."

"You're serious about everything," he pointed out. "But if we're being straightforward and honest with each other, I feel the need to share that I also had decided kissing you again wasn't a good idea."

"Oh." Was that disappointment trickling through her? How could it be? This was what she wanted. "Okay, then. We're both on the same page about this—"

"Not anymore. Now you've accused me of being a serial flirter. I'm feeling as if you just threw down the gauntlet, and my honor is at stake. Your declaration hits me as a challenge. A dare to see if I can do it again."

"No." She shook her head even as excitement coiled inside her. "That's not what I meant—"

Brandon stopped at the end of the table carrying two plates and their drinks, then set the appropriate items in front of each of them. "One Mama Bear. One Papa Bear. Cola with lemon and black coffee. Anything else I can get you?"

Maggie shook her head. All she wanted was to rewind and delete that ill-advised kiss and this whole conversation about it not happening again.

She'd just made everything worse.

Maggie glanced up from the spreadsheet on her computer monitor when the office door opened and Lucy Bishop walked in. "Hey, partner."

"Hey, yourself." The strawberry blonde lowered her skinny little self into one of the chairs in front of the desk. "You're back from lunch."

"Nothing gets by you." Maggie hoped the playful remark would cover her involuntary reaction to memories of that lunch. She felt a little shimmy in her tummy at the memory of Sloan's eyes when he'd all but said there would be another kiss. But now she was back at work and needed to get her head in the game.

"Did you have a good time?" Lucy asked.

"I did." Unfortunately, she had, but not in the "girl-friends catching up" way she'd expected. And that was really all she wanted to say about that. "How's everything in the café?"

"Good. We were busy today." She leaned back in the chair and sighed. "And I've been thinking."

"That's dangerous."

"You have no idea." Lucy grinned. "Seriously, though. Suddenly it's April and summer will be here before you

know it. That means tourists and—fingers crossed—a
jump in business, which we need to prepare for. We should
talk about possible additions and changes to the café menu
and an increase in supplies."

"Not to mention hiring extra staff," Maggie pointed out.

"Probably high school and college students looking for
summer jobs."

"I have a list of kids who worked in the ice cream parlor," Maggie said. "Most of them are smart and hard work-
ers. Conscientious. I can start making calls to see who
might be interested in coming back. Line up the standouts."

"It's going to be a tough call to decide how many we
need for the ice-cream side and the food-service side."

"A delicate balance, for sure," Maggie agreed.

"We have no idea how busy it's going to be our first
summer." There were shadows in Lucy's bright blue eyes.
"If we don't have enough staff, customers will be kept
waiting for food and not inclined to give us their repeat
business. But we don't want to pay employees for standing around doing nothing."

"Yeah, it's definitely a numbers-and-luck game," Maggie agreed. "I'm pretty sure the mayor's office keeps statis-
tics on summer visitors from year to year. We can probably
get a copy and work out a reasonable guess at the percent-
age of customers to expect. I'd be inclined to lowball the
staffing ratio. If we get swamped, I'll help out. And I have
some emergency reinforcements in mind."

"It's a good place to start." Lucy nodded. "Wow, I never
realized being the boss would be so hard. I'm very glad
we're in this together."

"Me, too."

Maggie remembered the pressure of handling just Potter's Ice Cream Parlor all alone. She and Danny had opened
it together. When his National Guard unit had been called

up and deployed to Afghanistan, her solo engagement had only supposed to have been temporary. Then he'd been killed in action and she was pregnant. All the responsibility of the business, as well as the baby, had fallen to her.

On top of that, or maybe because of the stress and trauma, there were complications with her pregnancy and the obstetrician ordered her to stay off her feet. If it hadn't been for friends and family, she would never have made it through that terrible time.

Lucy Bishop had been a summer visitor to Blackwater Lake a couple of years ago and fell in love with the town. She'd finished culinary school and eventually relocated, working at the Grizzly Bear Diner for a while. She and Maggie had become friends because Lucy had a notorious sweet tooth and was the best ice-cream-parlor customer.

She never said much about her background and Maggie still didn't know anything about her personal life. But she liked Lucy and was aware that she had a passion for cooking good healthy food. Instead of throwing out what they couldn't use at the end of the day, her friend made sure less fortunate people in town had enough to eat.

She'd confided to Maggie her dream of opening her own restaurant and then a couple of things had fallen into place. The shop space next to Maggie's business had become available and Lucy had inherited some money.

They had partnership papers drawn up and opened the Harvest Café last Labor Day weekend. At first, they'd broken even and revenue from the ice cream parlor, along with a busy winter season, had kept them afloat. Now they were making a small profit. This would be their first summer and, hopefully, it would be a good one.

Lucy looked thoughtful. "I've heard that the resort project is going to be constructed on two fronts simultaneously—

the condos at the base of the mountain at the same time as the hotel with retail shops a little farther up."

Sloan hadn't said anything to Maggie about that, but they didn't talk business. She'd been concentrating so hard on avoiding him and keeping conversation to a minimum that she never asked.

"If that's true," she said, "it could be really positive news for our business. You're talking a good-size work-force, and those people need to eat."

"Plus, more permanent and part-time residents will live here when the condos are finished. The hotel will cater to skiers in the winter and fishing and lake-oriented tourists in summer."

"That's true." Maggie leaned back in her chair. "Who told you about this? Is it a reliable source?"

"It was someone who works for McKnight Construction. One of the cabinetmakers, I think. He said Sloan Holden is bringing in his own contractor, who will coordinate with Alex McKnight."

"That would be great."

Maggie wondered if Sloan would be around until the project was completed. The scope of it was pretty big, which could keep him in Blackwater Lake for a long time. On the one hand, that would mean having a stable boarder and a reliable income source, which was important for paying her small-business loan. On the other hand, he could be under her roof indefinitely. That would make her life complicated.

"You could ask Sloan," Lucy suggested.

"About what?"

"How he's planning to approach the building project. After all, you see him every day. He lives in your house."

"True."

"So it seems like a reasonable question. When you see him at home," Lucy said.

"And sometimes not at home."

"Hmm. That sounds interesting. I sense a story there."

"Not really. I just ran into him at the diner. Jill cancelled because C.J. was sick. Sloan walked in while I was there and we had lunch together."

"So when you said it was good, that didn't exactly cover all the facts. How was it?" Lucy asked again. "You look a lot more relaxed than before you left."

Warmth crept into Maggie's cheeks. "I had a good time."

And, God help her, that was the truth. When Sloan walked into the diner, or any room for that matter, things were definitely not dull.

Lucy studied her. "Now that I think about it, there's something different about you. And I don't just mean because you're not the stressed-out partner I sent off to lunch with orders to have a good time."

"It was nice to get out for a little while." It was even nicer to know a man was interested enough in her not to take no for an answer in terms of another kiss. That was different from wanting him to kiss her. It was just nice to know a man thought she was attractive.

It had been a long time since any man had been interested and Maggie preferred it that way. She'd had her great love and had made peace with that. When Sloan got the message, he would be glad he was off the hook.

She noticed Lucy was looking at her funny. "What's wrong?"

"You're blushing." The other woman leaned forward in her chair. "Methinks there's more to this story."

"Not really."

"You should be aware that your answer has no conviction whatsoever."

"He's a flirt. That's all."

"Aha." Lucy nodded as if that explained everything.

"No aha," Maggie protested. "What does that mean anyway?"

"It means that you left here looking uptight and stressed out. My guess is that he's responsible for the fact that you are no longer looking as though you want to bend steel with your bare hands. You're glowing."

"No I'm not."

"I can get you a mirror." Lucy looked very certain of her observation. "You definitely are glowing."

"You make me sound as if I came in contact with radioactive material." Come to think of it, that wasn't far from the truth. Sloan was too hot for her to handle, even if she wanted to.

"It's just that I've never seen you look like this before. The only difference now is him." Lucy shrugged.

"That's weird because I don't feel any different. He rents a room from me. It's a mutually beneficial arrangement. Nothing more. We're barely even friends. He suggested we eat together only because he didn't want to sit at the diner counter and chat up a stranger behind it."

"Okay." But there was a gleam in her friend's eyes. "Then, I guess you wouldn't mind if I flirt with him a little?"

"Of course not." Maggie's tone was adamant—and automatic.

"Seriously? You have no objections to me going after him? And if he asks me out?"

"Absolutely none." That was stubbornness talking. "Go with my blessing."

"Okay, then." Lucy stood. "He is an exceptionally good-looking guy. And quite the charmer. If I get the chance, I'm going to let him know I'm interested."

"Remember, he's divorced." At her friend's questioning look, she added, "He told April, Delanie and I. Keep in mind that he might be disillusioned and have no intention of settling down."

"Good. Neither do I." She looked at her watch. "I have to get back downstairs."

"Okay. I'll see you later."

When Maggie was alone, she let out a long breath and felt like a two-faced witch. She'd given Lucy, her partner and friend, the okay to show interest in Sloan. The problem was, Maggie wasn't at all sure she meant it. Oh, God. Was she one of those friends? The "I can't have him but I don't want her to have him" kind of woman?

It would mean she had feelings for Sloan.

Chapter Six

Maggie parked in the lot at O'Keefe Technologies where her brother, Brady, had built the corporate headquarters for his company. He'd chosen a beautiful spot for it. From his office window he had a spectacular view of the mountains in the distance. If Maggie worked there, not much would be accomplished what with her looking out the window all day.

After getting out of the SUV, she walked toward the glass double-door entry and the hair on the back of her neck stood up. There was a parking area reserved for people who worked in the building, and she spotted Sloan's silver Range Rover.

It had been a week since their chance meeting at the diner. During that time she'd only seen him at the house for meals and hadn't really made more than small talk with him. Nothing like the intimate nature of their conversation at lunch.

Her skin had tingled and burned just talking with him about kissing. She really hoped to get in and out of the building without running into him, or anything else that would test her ultimatum about kissing him again.

She walked into the lobby and automatically looked at the directory, even though she knew that her brother's office was located on the fourth floor. The fifth was leased to Holden Property Development, where Sloan and his cousin Burke had their offices. Again her skin prickled just knowing Sloan was here somewhere. Part of her wanted to see him, but the survival-instinct part of her knew that wasn't a good idea.

Maggie pushed the elevator up button, and when the doors opened, a sigh of relief escaped her. Sloan hadn't taken this one to the lobby and she was getting off before his floor. She was halfway home free in Operation Avoid Sloan.

The car went up and the doors opened to a reception area where Olivia Lawson, her brother's executive assistant and fiancée, sat behind her desk. The pretty, blue-eyed blonde smiled warmly. "Hi, Maggie. How are you?"

"Great. You?"

"Fabulous. And how is that precious little girl of yours?"

"Good. But you know the terrible twos everyone talks about? It really is terrible." She shuddered, recalling that nightmarish trip to the grocery store then Sloan unexpectedly coming to her rescue.

"She has a mind of her own, doesn't she?" Her sister-in-law-to-be looked sympathetic.

"That's putting it mildly. Intellectually I know it's a good thing and just a speed bump on the road to independence, which is every parent's goal for their child." She sighed. "I just wish that the learning curve on this would play out somewhere private, where no one could see and give you a look that says you were nowhere to be found when maternal competence was being handed out."

"You're doing a fabulous job," Olivia protested. "Danielle is lucky you're her mom."

"You have to say that. You're marrying my brother and you want me to like you because I'm his sister."

"Busted." The other woman shrugged then grinned. "It's all about diplomacy and kissing up to the sister."

"I knew it." Nothing could be further from the truth.

"Seriously, Mags, when Brady and I have babies, I hope I'm even half as good a mom as you are."

Their kids would be lucky because the two of them would be a whole parenting team, Maggie thought, envying the couple. It was hard raising a child, but as the saying went, many hands made light work. Two against one had to be easier. She'd seen it herself the day Sloan had helped her with groceries and her little girl. As grateful as she'd been to him, the experience had left her with an empty and sad feeling that her daughter wouldn't know the security of having a father in her world.

"Speaking of babies, Danielle needs a cousin," she said. "When are you and Brady going to get on that whole baby-making thing?"

"Who's making babies?" That was her brother's voice.

Maggie hadn't noticed him in the doorway to his office. "Hi, big brother."

"Little sister." He walked over to hug her. "So who's making babies?"

"I'm hoping you and your beautiful bride-to-be."

He gave his fiancée a lecherous look. "We are practicing all the time."

"That's a very unsatisfactory answer," Maggie retorted.

"On the contrary—" he winked at Olivia, who was blushing "—it's very satisfying."

"Okay, then. Let me ask another question. No nuance, just yes or no. Have you set a date for the wedding?"

"As a matter of fact, we have." Brady had a smug look on his handsome face.

"Do you plan to share?" she asked.

"Olivia, you do the honors."

There was an adoring look in her eyes as she gazed at her fiancé. She'd looked at him like that a long time before Brady had realized that he was in love with her, too. "Saturday, June 25."

"Oh, my gosh. That's only a couple months." Maggie hugged Brady, then his fiancée. "That's fantastic. I'm so happy for you guys."

"And I have a favor to ask you," Olivia said. "Will you be my matron of honor?"

Maggie didn't know what it was about engagements and weddings, but tears filled her eyes and emotion choked off her words so that she could only nod. When she could finally speak, she said, "I would absolutely love that."

"And we want Danielle to be a flower girl." Brady put his arm around Olivia's waist.

"You do know that she'll only be two and a half and doesn't follow directions very well, if at all?"

"We don't care about that," her brother said. "She's our niece and we want her in the wedding."

Olivia nodded. "Whatever happens is fine. Everything she does is perfect to us. The best part is the spontaneous, adorable factor that will make our day unique and special."

Maggie's eyes filled with tears again when she looked at her brother. "You do know that Olivia is too good for you."

"I do," he said solemnly, then grinned as if he'd performed a new trick. "See? I'm already practicing."

"This news is so awesome," Maggie said. "Does Mom know?"

"Not yet. We're taking her to dinner tonight to break the news. You had to go and ask your yes-or-no question, so there was no dodging an answer. You'd have known something was up and hounded us until we broke." He pointed at her. "But if you spill it to Mom before we can, you'll be demoted from matron of honor to guest-book duty."

"My lips are sealed. This is so cool," she gushed.

Maggie was ecstatic for them. But she also felt the tiniest bit of envy and hated herself for it. They deserved every happiness. But she was only human and wished her life had worked out the way she'd planned.

"As much as I hate to kill the buzz," she said to her brother, "can I steal you away for a little work?"

"Right," Brady said. "You wanted to talk about updating your website."

"Yeah."

"No problem." He held out a hand, indicating she should go into his office. "Right this way."

"See you later, bride-to-be." She smiled at Olivia.

"Count on it. We have a lot to talk about and I'm going to need your help."

Maggie nodded, then followed her brother and he closed the office door behind them. There were two barrel-backed chairs facing his desk and she took the right one while he sat down behind the desk.

"What can I do for you?"

"Lucy and I were talking last week about the business. Our first summer since combining the ice cream parlor and café is coming up. With tourist season on the horizon, it's a good time to overhaul the website. We were too busy after the café launch to do it during the winter, but now things are running more smoothly."

"A new Facebook page wouldn't hurt, either," he said absently, typing on his keyboard.

"You're the computer guru, so I bow to your expertise and judgment. And hope you'll give me a break on your normally exorbitant charges."

"I should inflate my fee." Brady gave her a pointed look.

Maggie knew he was still smarting because she hadn't

come to him for a business loan, but decided to play innocent. "But you won't."

"Give me one good reason why not. I still haven't forgiven you for not consulting me before you decided to open a B and B to make payments. I could have helped with the financing."

"You know why I didn't," she protested. "If Danny were here, that's the way he would have handled it."

"And if he were still here, he'd be around in that house where you're renting rooms to strangers."

"It's working out great. Josie is a huge help and I love having her there."

"What about Sloan Holden?" he asked while staring at his computer monitor, where her current outdated website was displayed.

"He pays his rent on time and doesn't bring wild women back to his room."

Brady glanced at her. "What does that mean?"

"Just what I said. He's an ideal guest." Except for the inconvenient fact that he'd kissed her. But because of her part in it, she'd decided not to hold that against him.

Her brother's eyes narrowed on her. "He hasn't gotten out of line, has he?"

No, she thought, that would describe her. "He's very nice and I'm grateful to have the income."

Brady studied her for a moment then nodded. "So what changes are you looking for?"

"That's your area. What do you think I should change?"

"I can come up with a new design, but I'd suggest current pictures of you and Lucy that show both the ice cream parlor and café. April Kennedy can help you with that."

Maggie made a mental note to visit her photography studio just down the street from the café and across from the sheriff's office. "Okay, what else?"

"Put up menus for meals and desserts. Maybe a pairing like some restaurants do for wines. Advertise coupons, giveaways. Like kids-eat-free Mondays. Or two-for-one Tuesdays. Things like that."

"I'll talk to Lucy and pick her brain," Maggie promised.

"Then I think a little plug for Blackwater Lake as the perfect tourist destination," Brady said.

"That all sounds good."

"Okay. Get back to me as soon as possible with the material and I'll put it all together." He met her gaze. "No charge."

"Have I told you that you're the best brother in the whole world?"

"Yeah, yeah. Talk is cheap." There was phony little-boy petulance in his tone. "Actions speak louder than words."

"Don't be that way," she pleaded. "I know if I needed you that you'd be there for me and Danielle. But I found out how unpredictable life is when I lost Danny. That made me realize I need to do things on my own. Not count on anyone."

"I really do get it," he said gently. "But it's in the big brother's handbook to never miss a chance to needle your little sister."

"And you're very good at that." She smiled and stood up. After blowing him a kiss, she said, "I'll be in touch. Have fun with Mom tonight. Isn't it about quitting time?"

"You're my last appointment. Now get out of here so Liv and I can shut everything down and go pick up Mom."

"I'm so gone."

Maggie left his office and said goodbye to Olivia. She pushed the down button and when the doors opened, Sloan Holden was the sole occupant of the elevator.

A slow smile curved up the corners of his mouth. "This is an unexpected surprise."

Maggie wasn't often speechless. She took pride in being queen of the smart-aleck comeback or witty retort. She should have been prepared to see him and had been ready when she'd walked into the building. But wedding news pushed it out of her mind and now she had nothing. This was a particularly bad time to lose her words. Olivia was sitting right behind her and there was no way she wouldn't notice weird or unusual behavior in her matron-of-honor-to-be.

"Hi," she finally said, then walked into the elevator and watched the doors close.

"What brings you here? Just a wild guess—it has something to do with your brother."

"Yes." They stopped on the first floor and the elevator doors opened to the marble floor of the lobby. She stepped out. "I want to update my website and that's what Brady does. It's quite handy to have a computer nerd in the family."

"Is business good?"

"Very. And our plan is to give it a little nudge so it will be even better come summer."

"You and your partner must be pleased."

"We are."

"Your success doesn't surprise me. The food is great and the atmosphere friendly and inviting. Linking the café and ice cream parlor is smart. I can only speak for myself, but I'm never too full for ice cream."

That was so boyishly charming she couldn't help smiling. "I should get you to star in a commercial."

The elevator dinged and the doors opened. Burke Holden stepped out and smiled at them. The cousins were similarly built, and a facial resemblance pegged them as family. But Burke's eyes were vivid blue and his hair was a little lighter than Sloan's.

"Hi, Maggie." Burke exited the elevator and stopped beside her. He and his fiancée, Sydney McKnight, were frequent visitors to the café. "How are you?"

"Good. You?"

"Never better. On my way home to pick up Syd." He looked at Sloan. "Hey, you're still going to meet us for dinner, right?"

"That's the plan." He met her gaze. "I'm not sure how much notice my landlady needs that I won't be dining at the boardinghouse."

"No problem. It's spaghetti night."

"Maggie," Burke said, looking at her. "You should come, too. Syd would love to see you."

"I wish I could," she said politely. "But I don't have a babysitter for Danielle."

"Bring her along. I'm good with kids. Just ask Syd."

Maggie glanced at Sloan, who wasn't saying much, mostly looking interested in what she was going to say. Probably amused about how she would wiggle out of this invitation. Well, she would show him.

"It really sounds like fun. You're sure you don't mind a two-year-old at dinner?"

"Not at all. We'd love it."

"Have you ever had dinner in a restaurant with a two-year-old?"

"No," Burke answered. "But how bad can it be?"

"You'd be surprised," she said mysteriously. "I'll try to get a sitter, but…"

"If you can't, don't worry about it," Burke assured her. "We're going to a place near the mall and it's not fancy. With the lodge renovations, the Fireside Restaurant won't be back open for a while. Sloan has all the information. You guys should come together."

He waved, then headed for the double glass doors. She

and Sloan silently watched him walk out of the building before looking at each other.

"I sure hope he's not matchmaking, because you and I have already agreed that I'm not your type," she reminded him.

He smiled serenely. "Isn't it handy that I don't have to pick you up?"

Then he walked out the door and Maggie stood there alone, wondering what train had just mowed her down. Fate had a weird sense of humor, putting him on that down elevator at the same time she was getting on. And then Burke had found them chatting. Maggie had come here for a business meeting and was leaving with a dinner engagement.

She refused to call it a date.

"So you and Sloan?" Sydney McKnight was washing her hands in the ladies' room at Don Jose's, a Mexican restaurant about forty-five minutes from Blackwater Lake.

"It's not what you think," Maggie answered. "He's renting a room from me. We're friends. I think."

She and Sloan, along with Danielle, had met Syd and Burke at the restaurant. Strapped in the car seat, her daughter had napped the whole way and the two adults had chatted. It had been—nice. But that was all.

After being seated at a table, they'd ordered, then Sydney announced a trip to the powder room. The men had assumed Maggie would go, too, and teased them about women traveling together in platoons. So Maggie had taken them up on their offer to watch her toddler. Even though she knew Sydney was curious about her relationship with Sloan and, when they were alone, would grill her like a kebab.

So here they were in the ladies' room.

"Friends? You think? That's it?" Sydney persisted.

"Yes." Maggie glanced at her reflection in the mirror. The red sweater and black slacks looked good. Her brown hair was shiny and fell in layers past her shoulders in a flattering style. She was okay, but not in the same league as the models and actresses Sloan dated. "You know I like a romance as much as the next woman, but there just isn't one going on between Sloan and me."

Then it hit her that maybe Holden men didn't necessarily settle down with high-profile women. Sydney was a mechanic and worked with her dad at McKnight Automotive. She'd met Burke when he'd brought his car in for service and now they were engaged to be married. A beautiful brunette with dark eyes, she really cleaned up well in her skinny jeans, white silk blouse and red blazer. Burke didn't seem to care that she didn't have a glamorous profession. Theirs was a lovely romance and Maggie was happy for them. But before panic set in, she remembered that Sloan had enthusiastically agreed with Maggie that she wasn't his type.

"He's awfully good with your daughter." Syd brushed a smudge of mascara from beneath her left eye. "Not just any man would volunteer to watch her while her mom goes to the powder room."

Syd didn't know it, but this wasn't the first time he'd volunteered. That very first morning in her house he'd taken Danielle outside.

"He's great with her" was all she said.

"So he's good-looking. Nice. Funny. Charming. An eligible bachelor. And pretty decent father material. Where's the downside?" Syd folded her arms over her chest.

"It's obvious that you and Burke are in love. When that happens, you want to see everyone around you in love, too.

But maybe a relationship isn't the right thing for someone else," she said gently.

"You're talking about you," Syd said.

Maggie shrugged. "Everyone's path is different. Sloan might be a wonderful husband and father, but not for me or Danielle. It's my job and mine alone to raise her the way her father would have wanted."

"I hear what you're saying." Syd nodded her understanding. "But I knew Danny and he was a good man. He used to bring the cars into the garage all the time, so we got to know each other pretty well. I'm not so sure he would have minded another good man stepping in when he couldn't be there for his wife and daughter."

Maggie couldn't say the other woman was wrong about that. Because of his military service, Danny faced danger the average man didn't. He thought about things other husbands and fathers didn't have to. Just before his final deployment, he'd asked her if she would remarry should something happen to him. She'd tried to make light of it, never really believing he wouldn't come home. She'd said something glib about not wanting to train another man, but Danny had been serious. He'd told her he trusted her and to do what was right for her and the baby. All he wanted was for her to be happy.

Maggie knew the deeper issue was *her*. "The thing is, I'm going to have to be enough for my little girl because I don't want another romance. Not ever again."

"You obviously loved him very much. I'm sorry, Maggie. I didn't mean to push." There was regret in Syd's dark eyes.

"It's okay."

"No, it isn't, but you're sweet to say that." The other woman shook her head. "And I understand. Everyone's past puts them in a place where they're open to love. Or not."

"Right." It was a lonely place not being open, Maggie

thought, but that was where she was. "I'm starting to feel guilty about being gone this long."

"I'm sure Danielle is fine with Burke and Sloan."

"They're the ones I'm worried about."

Syd laughed, and any tension, real or imagined, disappeared. "It's good for them."

"Builds character," Maggie agreed.

They left the ladies' room and walked over the tile floor through the restaurant decorated like a Mexican hacienda. The walls were painted to look like adobe and had sombreros hanging on them. Sloan and Burke were seated at a table for four with a high chair for Danielle. Maggie always carried antiseptic wipes in the diaper bag and had thoroughly cleaned the chair before putting her daughter in it.

She wasn't in it when they returned to the table, because Sloan was holding her and looking as if he didn't mind.

Maggie stood on the other side of the high chair. "Is she fussy?"

"No. Good as gold," he said.

"Does she need a diaper change?"

He looked at the child in his arms. "I'm no expert, but she seems fresh as a daisy. Right, Shorty?"

Danielle nodded, but Maggie figured he had this little girl so completely charmed that if he said, "Let's jump off a bridge," she would enthusiastically agree.

"So she hasn't been a problem at all?"

"No. She just held out her arms and I felt sorry for her all restricted in that contraption," Sloan explained.

"You are a completely spineless pushover." Syd gave him a pitying look, then her gaze rested on Burke. "Does that spineless streak run in the family? Will our children have you wrapped around their tiny little fingers?"

"No." His tone was adamant. Then he looked at the little girl and his expression grew soft. "Yes."

"Which is it?" Sloan was unselfconsciously holding Danielle in her long-sleeved pink dress, white tights and Mary Janes. She had ribbons in her hair. "Yes or no?"

"Maybe." Burke shrugged. "I will rationally assess each situation and react to it in whatever way my wife says I should."

"Oh, please. You're so full of it," Syd scoffed. "You've done a great job with Liam, which is more parenting experience than I've got."

"Where is he tonight?" Sloan asked.

"At his friend Todd's house," Syd said. His mother, Violet, was her best friend. They'd had a falling-out when Syd's boyfriend had fallen in love with Violet and eloped, but the two women had put it behind them and now the boys were besties. "We gave him a choice and he said he'd rather put up with Bailey, Todd's little sister, than a bunch of grown-ups." She shrugged. "What can I say? He's ten."

"Ouch." Sloan looked at Danielle. "How old will you be when having dinner with anyone over ten is worse than a root canal?"

"She probably feels that way right now," Maggie said, "but she can't verbalize it yet. I swear there are times when she looks at me and is thinking, 'If I could talk and dial the phone, Grandma would get an earful and you'd be sorry you didn't give me a *c-o-o-k-i-e*.'"

They all laughed, including Danielle, who clapped her hands for good measure.

"She is really cute," Burke said.

"Are you feeling your biological clock ticking?" Syd teased.

"Not the clock so much," he answered seriously. "Just that I'd really like having a mini-you."

"Aw." She touched his arm and the love shining in her eyes was obvious. "You're a keeper."

Sloan studied the child then looked at Maggie. "Speaking of minis... She looks a lot like you."

"That's the consensus," she agreed. "Poor kid."

"I don't think so." Sloan met her gaze and there was something in his eyes that sent a shiver down her spine. "Before you know it, boys are going to notice, and then you'll have your hands full."

"Don't remind me."

Just then a waiter arrived with a tray full of steaming plates. Sloan put Danielle back in the high chair as if he'd been doing it for years and the child went without protest. What was wrong with this picture?

Maggie hadn't tried very hard to find a babysitter. She'd secretly hoped her daughter would make dinner a challenge like any respectable two-year-old would. Not that she wanted to spoil Burke and Syd's evening. Her plan had been to take the fussy toddler outside, but it would be a warning to Sloan if he had any illusions about tempting her into a fling.

But if there was anything a mother could count on, it was that a child would make a liar out of her. Tonight was no exception. Her little girl had been practically perfect, the poster child for any couple considering whether or not to have children.

It turned out to be a wonderful evening. If there was a downside, it had to do with her and feelings that scratched at the wall she'd put up around her heart when her husband died. This was where she reminded herself that it wasn't just about her. She had to think about Danielle. Anything casual with a man was out of the question.

There were many things in life Maggie couldn't control, but getting involved with Sloan wasn't one of them.

Chapter Seven

After work Sloan returned to Maggie's house and went straight to his room via the outside stairway. As a paying guest, he had a kcy to the front door but preferred to come in the back way. Especially for the past three weeks, after taking Maggie and Danielle to dinner with Burke and Sydney.

They'd had a great time—at least he had. That little two-year-old charmer could wrap herself around his heart if he wasn't careful. And so could her beautiful mom. But if Burke hadn't invited them, Sloan certainly wouldn't have asked them along. It fell into personal territory. Every time the scales tipped in that direction, Maggie nudged him back over the line into neutral, and he didn't do neutral very well. It made him want to shake her up—in a very personal way.

All he had to do was look at her and he wanted to get very personal. But the woman had emotional baggage and he didn't want to unpack it, so he was keeping his distance—hence he was using his outside access to get to his room. That way he didn't have to see Maggie until dinner, and avoiding her seemed best for both of them.

He dropped off the paperwork he planned to look at later and changed out of his suit. He was a jeans and T-shirt kind of guy at heart, but sometimes a suit and tie was required.

Now he was at loose ends. After a long day, he wanted a break before diving into more work. He wondered if Josie was watching TV in the upstairs family room. After exiting his room, he walked down the hall to the garage-size common area and found it empty.

"She must be downstairs." Great. Talking to himself. That was why he needed someone else to talk to. And going to the first floor meant seeing Maggie. "At least Josie and Danielle will take the pressure off."

When he was alone with Maggie, his willpower and common sense seemed to go missing in action.

Sloan descended the stairs and wondered what was going on. It was way too quiet. Until rooming here at Potter House, quiet had always been his preference, but he'd gotten used to background noise. Right now there was a disquieting, no pun intended, lack of it. No female voices exchanging the latest town gossip. No screeching, chattering or crying from Shorty. In the six weeks he'd been here this had never happened.

At the bottom of the stairs Sloan heard noises but couldn't identify them. He walked through the great room and didn't see anyone, then got closer to the kitchen—and sounds he still couldn't place. After rounding the island, he saw Maggie. She was on her back, half in and half out of the cupboard underneath the sink. It happened to be a great view of her legs, and he felt that familiar tightening in his gut.

He was pretty sure she hadn't heard him and didn't want to startle her. Quietly he said, "Hi, Maggie."

"Sloan? Oh, gosh. I didn't know you were here already. What time is it?"

"Almost six."

"Rats," she mumbled.

"I can leave," he offered.

"No. I just lost track of time trying to deal with this stupid thing."

Now that he wasn't quite so preoccupied with the shape of her legs in those snug jeans, he noticed there was an open pink toolbox on the floor beside her. Next to that was a brown box containing a new faucet. It looked to him as if she was planning to replace the existing fixture.

"Is there a problem?" he asked.

"Leaky spigot."

"Have you ever changed one before?"

"It never dripped before."

She'd said her husband had built the house, and it was probable that all of the plumbing fixtures were original. "How old is this place?"

"Let me think." She grunted and there was a noise that sounded like a metal tool hitting bottom inside the cabinet. "Hell and damnation!"

"Are you all right?"

"Yes. Sort of." She wiggled her way out from under the sink, holding her left hand.

"What happened?" He went down on one knee beside her and saw blood.

"The wrench slipped. I tried to catch it. A sharp edge caught my finger."

"Let me take a look," he offered.

"I'm sure it's fine. I'll just put a bandage on it, then get dinner—"

"That can wait." He met her gaze. "Let me see your hand."

She stared at him for several moments, then correctly realized that he wasn't going to back off. She opened her right hand and he could see a gash on her left index finger that was oozing blood.

"Where are the clean dish towels?" he demanded.

"Top drawer next to the sink."

He reached over and opened it, grabbed a terry-cloth towel and pressed the material onto the wound. "I don't think it's deep. The bleeding should stop in a minute." He settled their hands on his thigh and saw something flicker in her eyes.

"I'm sure it's fine." And there was the push back to neutral land. But the words came out a little breathy. "I need to get dinner on the table."

"Maybe Josie can help," he suggested.

"She's not here. Dinner plans."

That explained why he hadn't heard them talking, but not the lack of little-girl activity. "Where's Danielle? Napping?"

"My mom has her."

So he was alone with Maggie. That was inconvenient. And Sloan was pretty sure his pulse spiked as the implications of it all sank in.

"Let me guess. You had a window of opportunity without a toddler around and decided to tackle a DIY project."

"Good guess," she said.

He lifted the towel to check her finger and missed the sensation of her hand on his thigh. "It's still bleeding a little, but I don't think it needs stitches."

"Sloan, I can take care of this."

"Probably. But it's not easy to bandage yourself with only one good hand." All he wanted to do was help and she brought down the cone of independence. It was annoying and offended his sense of chivalry. He didn't give her a choice but kept her injured hand in his and stood, then curved his fingers around her upper arm to help her stand.

"It's really not that big a deal."

"So give me two minutes to patch you up. Do you have peroxide, Band-Aids and antibiotic cream?"

"Yes." She nodded toward the upper cupboard by the sink.

"Okay. Hold this while I get everything."

Surprisingly she did as ordered without argument. He set the supplies on the granite, then took her hand and lifted the towel. "Looks as if the bleeding stopped."

"I concur."

"I'm going to hold your hand under the water to wash it off, then pour the peroxide on it. After that, ointment and a Band-Aid."

"Yeah. I kind of figured that." She smiled.

"Right." Their eyes met and it felt too much like a moment, so he got busy.

He turned on the faucet and saw a stream of water squirting out from the base of the spigot. "Ah, I can see why this needs changing."

"Yeah. The guy at the hardware store said it would be a piece of cake. I don't know what kind he eats, but he was dead wrong about this job." There was frustration and annoyance in her voice.

As promised, Sloan poured the cleansing agent over the gash and watched it bubble for several moments. Then he took a paper towel and blotted the moisture so the bandage would stick. He finished up the job and met her gaze.

"You're good as new," he said.

"Thank you. Wish I could say the same about my faucet."

"What's the problem? In changing it, I mean."

"The bolts holding the old one in place are on really tight. I couldn't budge them."

"Let me give it a try."

She shook her head with a bit more enthusiasm than necessary. "You're a paying guest. I can't ask you to do that."

"You didn't ask. I offered."

"And I appreciate that." She thought for a moment. "But if you were staying at Blackwater Lake Lodge and there was something wrong with the faucet in your bathroom, would you offer to help change it?"

"Probably not," he said.

"Okay, then. This is my problem and I will handle it. Until the plumber can fit me in, I'll have to live with it." She shrugged.

"In the meantime, that fixture is wasting water. I'm a green builder and well aware that water is life and saving it is important."

"I couldn't agree more. I'll get someone out here to fix it first thing tomorrow."

"A plumbing professional is a good idea."

"Why?" There was uneasiness in her eyes, as if she expected the other shoe to fall.

"If this one needs attention, there's a better than even chance that they all do."

"Is there a problem with the one in your room?"

"Not yet."

Her expression turned stubborn. "And the master bathroom is fine."

"I wouldn't know. I've never been in your bedroom."

Sloan gave himself a mental slap as soon as the words were out of his mouth. For days he'd been keeping his distance from her and everything had been fine. But something about the way she deflected him at every turn tapped into his stubborn streak and pushed him into baiting her.

It happened this time, too.

Her dark eyes flashed with temper and something else hot and exciting. Something smoky and sexy. "If you're looking for an invitation, you'll be waiting for a very long time."

She was saying he would never be invited into her bed. Just like the promise she'd made that hell would freeze over before she kissed him again.

"That sounds like another challenge, Maggie."

Her full lips pressed into a straight line for a moment. "You can twist my words any way you want, but we agreed that the idea of anything serious between us just isn't very smart."

"Maybe intelligent choices are highly overrated."

"Not for me," she said quietly. "I have Danielle to think about. Every choice I make is with her welfare in mind."

As it should be, he thought. "You're a terrific mother, Maggie."

"Thanks."

"And really, while I'm here, I don't mind helping you out when you need a little muscle."

"I appreciate that." She smiled and the tension was gone.

But it would be back unless somehow he could get a handle on his tendency to tease and challenge her.

Maggie walked into her mom's house without knocking. It was where she'd grown up and coming here was completely natural and normal.

After shutting the door, she called out, "Hi, Mom."

"In the family room, sweetie." The voice was soft and that meant her daughter had fallen asleep.

She walked past the living and dining rooms, which were across from each other, then into the family room that was open to the kitchen. Maureen O'Keefe was sitting on her floral sofa in front of the flat-screen TV where an animated movie was showing. As suspected, Danielle was asleep beside her.

Maggie looked tenderly at her daughter then bent to kiss her mother's cheek. "Thanks for watching her. Sorry I'm so late picking her up."

"Did you get the faucet changed?"

"No."

Since it was her mother's regular day to watch Danielle, Maggie had called to ask if she could give the little girl dinner. The project would have been impossible with a toddler climbing all over her under the sink. As it turned out, the project was impossible anyway. Mostly because she refused to let Sloan help.

"What happened?" her mom asked.

"The bolts holding the fixture in place were on so tight I couldn't budge them."

Sloan had offered his muscle, and since then all she could think about was what he looked like with his shirt off. Her imagination went out of control picturing his broad chest, muscular arms and that made her want to touch...

"Maggie?"

"Hmm?" She blinked away the seductive vision in her head and tried her best to focus.

"Did you hear what I said?" There was the mom voice Maureen had always used when she wanted undivided attention from her children.

"I confess," Maggie said. "My mind was wandering."

Dark eyes very like her own assessed her. "Did your mind wandering have anything to do with Sloan Holden?"

Maggie sat down at the end of the sofa with Danielle between them. It was a calculated action designed to stall the conversation and give her time to come up with an answer that would end this third degree.

She didn't want to talk about Sloan because it would make her feelings bigger than they were, give them more importance than she wanted them to have. By the same token, lying to her mother was something that wouldn't end well. Maggie knew this for a fact because she'd tried it as a child and the woman *always* knew. It didn't matter that she was now a grown woman. Telling Mom a falsehood flirted with bad karma.

The best she could come up with was a flanking maneuver. "Sloan rendered first aid when I hurt myself with the wrench." She held up her bandaged index finger.

"Is it bad?" The stern look slipped from her mom's face, replaced by maternal concern.

"No. Superficial. He didn't think I needed stitches and it's not bleeding anymore."

"Good. So if he was there to patch you up, why didn't you ask him to help get the old faucet off?"

"Oh, you know." *Think, Maggie.* How could she lie without telling a lie? Nothing succeeded like the truth. She had just the thing. "He's a high-powered executive with a multimillion-dollar company. A man like him doesn't get his hands dirty."

"Did you ask him for help?"

"Of course not. He's a paying guest. I couldn't ask him to do that. I'd look like the world's most unprofessional bed-and-breakfast owner. Not a reputation I want to have."

"I see your point." When her granddaughter sighed in her sleep, Maureen smiled softly. "So did he offer to help?"

Crap. This was a yes-or-no question. Not an inch of wiggle room. "Yes. I really need to get Danielle home—"

"Not so fast." Her mom held up a hand to stop her. "You've been tap dancing since I mentioned his name. What's up with that?"

"Nothing." *Liar, liar, pants on fire.*

"I don't believe you, but let's leave that for the moment. I'm more curious about the fact that he offered to help and you turned him down when you were so determined to get that job done. Why would you do that?"

"Like I said, Mom, it would be unprofessional because he's a paying guest at my bed-and-breakfast. I'll call the plumber." It would be highly unlikely that Harvey Abernathy, a fifty-year-old happily married father of two, would say anything about getting an invitation into her bedroom.

Her mom's eyes narrowed. "You turned down his help because you wanted him to kiss you again."

"How in the world did you get that from what I just said?" No matter that it was true.

"Maggie…" Her mother smiled at her the way she had at her granddaughter just a minute before. "You're a mother now. How did you know when your child was thirsty or hungry before she could talk even a little? Or when she needs reassurance or just to be left alone? Or when she's not feeling well even before there are signs that she's sick?"

Maggie shrugged. "Don't know how. I just do."

"And I just know, too, because I know you. Kissing Sloan was lovely in the moment, but then it felt uncomfortable and for that reason you're pushing him away."

Maggie wondered when she would learn not to question the power of maternal mind reading. "You're right. I'm not comfortable with all this man/woman weirdness. It's been a few weeks and nothing more happened with him."

"Are you disappointed or relieved?"

"Both," Maggie admitted. "It was exciting and that's tempting. But then I realized it's a bad idea on many levels and figured he did, too. Then when I refused his help, he pointed out that it was probably a good idea to get a plumber and have him check out all the fixtures because they're original and might need work."

"He's right."

"Maybe. But during this discussion I pointed out that

the one in my bedroom was fine. He said he wouldn't know about that because he's never been in my bedroom. And I said if he was waiting for an invitation he'd be waiting a long time."

"Oh, dear..."

"Yeah. He said that sounded a lot like I was challenging him to take me to bed." She hated to admit it, but getting her there wouldn't be much of a challenge.

"He's obviously interested in you, sweetie." There were questions and a whole lot of concern in her mother's eyes.

"I get that, Mom. But I can't trust it." Or herself, for that matter. "And I'm not looking."

"You're sure?"

"I missed Daddy when he died." Maggie would never forget that awful day when her father had collapsed in this house. It had been a massive heart attack and suddenly he was gone. For a long time this place had felt sad and lonely but that had passed and laughter had come back. "I know you were devastated after losing the man you loved. And you never remarried. I lost Danny suddenly, so if there's anyone who understands why you didn't, it's me."

There was a sad look in her mother's eyes. "So pushing Sloan away has nothing to do with the fact that he uses women, then discards them like tissues?" Her mother shrugged. "After you told Josie and me about that kiss we Googled him."

"His reputation is a consideration," Maggie admitted.

"Doesn't it just suck that the first man you're attracted to since your husband died is—how did you phrase it? Oh, yes, all flirt and no depth. A playboy."

"Yes, there are pictures and stories verifying that he has been photographed with many women." The statement neither confirmed nor denied that she was attracted to Sloan.

"I'm so torn, sweetie. On one hand I'm glad there's a

man in the house and you, Danielle and Josie aren't there all alone. Call me old-fashioned, but in my day women weren't so hell-bent on proving they can run the world without a man." She sighed. "On the other hand, I wish he looked like a garden gnome and had the personality of a troll."

"I see you've met him," Maggie teased.

"You bet. I stopped by your brother's office on the pretext of him taking me to lunch, then insisted he introduce me to Sloan." Suddenly her mother looked fierce, ready to rip someone's head off. Possibly Sloan's. "He's handsome, wealthy and has too much charm for my peace of mind. That makes me nervous for you."

"Don't worry, Mom. I'll be careful."

"Sometimes being careful isn't enough. That type of man can draw you in before you even know what's happening. He's a wolf and you're a vulnerable widow."

She was a widow. That was a fact. But vulnerable? Not so much. She could tell the good guys from the bad. Maggie felt the most ridiculous urge to defend him. Or throw herself at him. The complete opposite of what her mom was telling her to do.

What was she? Sixteen? Where was this rebellion coming from?

"It's getting late, Mom. I need to get my baby girl home now."

"I hate to see you wake her. Are you sure you don't want to leave her here tonight?"

"Thanks, but no. You've got your volunteer work at the library tomorrow with Josie. It's better if I keep to her morning routine."

"Okay. Everything's packed up in the diaper bag. Her shoes are in there, too."

Maggie thought about that. "I don't think I'll put them

on her. It will be hard enough not to wake her when I slip her sweater on. Then there's getting her in the car seat. If she sleeps through that, it will be a miracle. After this nap, if she wakes up, she won't be ready for bed until midnight."

And that would be Maggie's penance for not accomplishing the mission for which she'd asked her mother to babysit. If she'd taken Sloan up on his offer, that new faucet would be in. But she might have ended up with the playboy in her bed.

Danielle stirred but didn't awaken when Maggie picked her up, slid the diaper bag over her shoulder and headed for the front door.

Her mother opened it and smiled lovingly at both of them. "Good night, baby girl."

"Thanks again, Mom. I don't know what I'd do without you." She kissed the woman's cheek. "I love you."

"Love you, too."

On the drive to her house, Maggie thought about the conversation with her mom and her own defiant reaction. Maybe it was knee-jerk, a habit of pushing back because her mother was always right. That would imply this time she hoped Maureen was wrong.

Did the reaction have anything to do with how close Maggie was to crossing a line with Sloan? If she did, there was no going back. So staying far from that line seemed like the best plan.

The truth was that she wouldn't have to work very hard to keep her distance after the inhospitable way she'd behaved when he'd offered his help. It was unlikely he would be inclined to ask her out.

That thought was far more disappointing than it should be.

Chapter Eight

Sloan was in position behind a lectern that faced a packed town hall in order to give a presentation to the chamber of commerce and all interested citizens about the virtues of green building. The standing-room-only crowd was proof that these people really cared about their town, and he was here to convince them that he did, too.

He didn't have time right now to wonder about the why of it, but in this capacity crowd Maggie was the first person he spotted. Had he subconsciously been searching only for her? What with leaving before breakfast and not returning until late, he hadn't seen her for a few days. He'd been putting a lot of hours in preparing this talk. It was important to convince the community to trust him. That he was committed to reducing the environmental impact in building a project that would benefit the town.

And it was time to start.

"Good evening, ladies and gentlemen. For those of you who don't know me, my name is Sloan Holden. I'm with the Holden Development Company and in charge of construction on the condominium, hotel and retail resort project." He looked around the room, then let his gaze rest on Maggie, sitting on a folding chair, dead center in the third row. "It's obvious from this amazing turnout that each and every one of you is intensely interested in the project and how it will affect your town and quality of life here in Blackwater Lake."

As he gazed around the room, he saw people in the audience nodding their agreement. "I've provided a packet of information so you can follow my remarks and take it with you for further review at your leisure.

"What's new about green building is that costs can be the same, or less, than building a conventional structure with far less consequences for the environment. When you consider the energy savings, construction quality and lower maintenance over time, a sustainable building really is paying you back. This will benefit businesses that lease retail space and condominium owners.

"But I suspect most of you are here to get a sense of how this venture will impact the mountain site and the breathtaking scenery surrounding it. Holden Development specializes in minimizing site impact and construction waste. That starts with a design that uses less land. We've hired a local architect. I'm sure most of you know Ellie McKnight, and her work is brilliant. Who has more skin in the game than someone who lives right here in Blackwater Lake?"

Sloan went on for another fifteen minutes explaining the company's objective of conserving energy and natural resources. He'd worked hard to include the right amount of detail and information but not so much that it would make their heads explode.

"In conclusion, I want to assure you that we are committed to building smart, building green. Not only to preserve the beauty and natural resources here, but in a global way."

He looked around, trying to gauge the reaction, and again his gaze settled on Maggie. Big mistake. That pretty face made him think about kissing her, and he couldn't afford to be distracted.

"There's more information in the material I provided, including the phone number of my office. If there are any questions after you've thoroughly reviewed everything, feel free to contact me. Also, I encourage everyone to research Holden Development. I'm confident our outstanding reputation will withstand intense scrutiny and ease any misgivings. Thank you for your time and attention."

There was polite applause and then Sloan gathered up his notes from the lectern. Mayor Loretta Goodson-McKnight made a few remarks in support of the building project before ending the meeting. With so many people standing at the back of the room, it took a few minutes for the rows of people in the chairs to file out toward the rear exit.

In the center aisle, Sloan was waiting his turn to merge with everyone. As it happened, that turned out to be perfect timing. He was there just as Maggie made her way to the end of her row.

"Hi." He held his hand out. "After you."

"Thanks." She smiled and moved in front of him.

And there it was, that tightening in the gut that always happened whenever she was near. Somehow it seemed stronger tonight. Maybe because he hadn't seen her for a few days. Even so, that didn't mean he could get her out of his thoughts.

He'd really missed the sound of her voice, the scent of her skin. The way her eyes sparkled. Her sense of humor. From where he stood, there was a pretty nice view of her sunny yellow cardigan, faded blue jeans and navy flats. Those jeans hugged the curve of her butt in the best possible way.

Finally they made it outside, where the cool, fresh air chilled the heat his thoughts had generated. "Where are you parked?"

"In the lot by city hall," she said.

He knew it was a couple blocks from here. "Me, too. Mind if I walk with you?"

"No."

He'd half expected her to shut him down and was glad she hadn't. Above them, old-fashioned streetlights illuminated the sidewalk in front of the town's community center. People headed in different directions, so the crowd was melting away. The echo of voices faded and soon there was just the sound of their footsteps on concrete.

Sloan fell into step next to her, walking on the street side. "What did you think of my presentation?"

"Very informative." She glanced up at him and the moonlight revealed her teasing smile. "On the plus side, I didn't hear anyone around me snoring."

"Ouch. That boring?" He slid his right hand into his slacks pocket to minimize the temptation of linking his fingers with hers. "Or are you mocking me?"

"What do you think?"

"I think I don't want to know," he said.

"Actually, you did a good job of giving the facts without too much embellishment. Short and sweet." She held up the packet of material that had been handed out. "This was a good move. If anyone wants to know more, they can read it or Google Holden Development as you suggested. Because everyone absorbs information differently."

"How so?"

"Some people are auditory and a speech works for them. Some are visual and need to read things in order to internalize it. I'm one of those."

"Oh?" He liked that she seemed in the mood to talk, and he was content to listen, hear the sound of her voice.

"And here's an example. Have you ever made the mistake of agreeing to take one of those phone surveys?"

"Can't say that I have."

"Right," she said drily. "You have a layer of protection from annoying calls. Okay. I'll explain. Someone asks you to take a survey, then reads several paragraphs and wants you to evaluate it on a scale of one to ten, one being very likely and ten being highly unlikely. By the time they're finished reading, I can't even remember the rating system."

"I'll have to tell my assistant never to put one of those calls through to me."

She laughed. "I suspect she doesn't really need a directive from you."

"Probably not." Still, as someone who'd lived here all her life, he valued her opinion and wanted her thoughts on tonight. "How do you think the audience in general responded?"

"Favorably. The people around me were smiling and nodding." She looked up at him. "But they were women who could just be taken in by your charm and good looks."

"You think I'm charming?"

She turned right into the city hall parking lot. "Do you really want me to answer that? Are you a quart low on ego?"

"Maybe." He laughed and realized that was what he'd missed most. Her making him laugh.

"All I'll say is that you are pleasant company." She stopped by the familiar SUV. "Here's my car."

Sloan realized he wasn't ready to give up her company and go back to the impersonal landlady/boarder existence they'd settled into. He wanted to talk to her, but the idea of asking her to spend time with him was a little nerve-racking. It felt a lot like being a teenager and asking a girl you had a crush on to the prom.

Maybe he *was* a little low on ego.

All she could do was say no.

"Would you like to get a quick bite to eat before going back to the house? Or a drink if you already had dinner?"

She had her keys out but stopped before pressing the button on the fob that would unlock the doors. Hesitantly, she met his gaze.

When a few seconds passed without an answer, he filled the silence and gave her an out if she wanted one. "You probably have to get back to Danielle."

"Actually, Josie is with her. And I didn't have a chance to eat before the meeting." She smiled and said, "I'm pretty hungry."

He was, too, but not necessarily for food. Being with Maggie in the moonlight brought back memories of kissing her and the yearning to do it again. "Good."

"Really? You're happy that I'm starving and could eat a horse?"

"No. Of course not. I just meant good that you want to have something to eat with me." Dear God, now he sounded like an overeager, inexperienced teenager in addition to feeling like one.

"I know what you meant." She thought for a moment. "What about Bar None? It will be less crowded than the diner and no one under twenty-one is allowed inside. Don't get me wrong, I adore my daughter, but on the rare occasions she's not with me, it's kind of nice to go somewhere only grown-ups are allowed."

"Bar None it is." He opened her car door for her. "See you there."

"Okay." She smiled and shut herself inside.

Sloan jogged to his car; he was in a hurry. Partly because he was looking forward to seeing her, but mostly because he was afraid she would change her mind.

But ten minutes later they were sitting at a bistro table in the establishment on Main Street. Cardboard menus stood up on the table and they each took one. He studied the listed items and still managed to glance at Maggie when she wasn't looking. She probably wouldn't make the list of the world's ten most beautiful women, unlike most of the ones he'd dated, but there was something about her that drew him.

"I think I'll have the soup-and-salad combo," she said. "And a glass of white wine."

"A sensible choice."

There was a twinkle in her eyes when she said, "I bet you're going for the B and B—burger and beer."

"What gave me away?"

"It was the sensible part. And the fact that you're a guy."

Just then, a waitress came over and took their orders. She told them she'd be back with their drinks and the food was coming right up. Then they were alone again.

"What does being a guy have to do with ordering a hamburger?" he asked.

"Don't forget the sensible part. It implies that you are fully aware of more nutritional choices you could make. But nine times out of ten a man will get red meat and the only hint of healthy is the lettuce, tomato and onion that comes on it."

"You do realize that's negatively profiling men," he pointed out.

"Profiles exist for a reason. Think about your guy friends. Tell me I'm wrong."

"It's as if you're psychic," he teased.

"Hardly. Danny used to—" Suddenly she stopped, as if she'd just revealed national secrets, and all the merriment disappeared. The expression on her face could only be described as guilt. "Never mind."

If it would help, he would encourage her to talk about the husband she'd lost. Because after she mentioned him, the carefree young woman who'd been enjoying herself was gone.

He might be a selfish bastard, but Sloan wanted that young woman back.

Maggie had always enjoyed busy, mindless chores like cutting up vegetables for the following morning's omelets. Tonight she realized it gave her too much time to think. She was doing that now as she put sliced mushrooms into a container, then pressed the lid on it.

She should never have accepted Sloan's dinner invitation.

He'd caught her at a weak moment. The problem was that every moment around Sloan made her weak. Not only that, she hadn't been ready when he'd asked her to get a bite to eat. She'd been so sure that he wouldn't waste any more time on her. Then he'd surprised her and the word *yes* had come out of her mouth before she could think it through.

At Bar None things had been going well. She'd been relaxed and that was when it happened. She'd started to tell Sloan that Danny had never listened to her warnings about limiting hamburgers. It felt wrong to talk to another man about him, especially because she felt something for Sloan. But it was as if she'd turned her back on her husband. If she and Sloan hadn't already ordered food, she would have made an excuse and walked out. A hasty exit would have been better than the awkward conversation that had followed. Still, it was her punishment for saying yes in the first place.

The only thing that saved her more awkwardness on the drive home was having her own car. Sloan had followed her, and when they'd arrived at the house, he'd said good-night and used the outside stairs to go to his room.

Danielle was peacefully sleeping and Josie had gone to bed. Maggie was alone and couldn't shut off her thoughts.

"Maggie, I—"

"Dear God—" She started at the unexpected male voice behind her. Her pulse throbbed when she turned around to face Sloan. "You scared me."

"Sorry. Next time I'll whistle. Or clear my throat. Or something."

"Yeah. Something."

She saw that he'd changed out of his expensive dark suit and silk, charcoal tie. The jeans and cotton shirt with its sleeves rolled up made him look every bit as attractive. Sexy, in a rugged way. That just proved dangerous thinking could happen even when you were cutting up vegetables.

They stared uneasily at each other for several moments, then finally she remembered he was a paying guest. She'd freshened his room that morning and replaced the towels.

"Is there something you need?"

"Yes."

"I'll get it for you right away. How can I help you?"

"You can talk to me." He moved closer, stopping at the kitchen island that separated them. His light brown eyes darkened and began to smolder as he stared at her.

Her heart started pounding again and it had nothing to do with being startled. He didn't want to discuss sheets, towels, the B and B's choice of body lotion or lack of a chocolate on his pillow. This was personal and didn't come under the heading of hospitality.

"It's late, Sloan. I have a busy day tomorrow and you probably do, too. Can we talk another time?"

"I'd prefer to have a conversation now. If you don't mind." He folded his arms over his chest. "While you're vulnerable."

"Excuse me?"

"It's not what you're thinking. I'd never take advantage of you. But I need to understand what happened tonight at Bar None." He didn't look confused as much as determined not to let her off the hook.

"Okay." She gave him points for being straightforward. It was a little unexpected, given his well-publicized dating history. "But I'm not sure what you mean about something happening tonight."

"Have you ever heard the expression when you bury your head in the sand you leave your backside exposed?"

"No. But I get it."

"Do you?" he challenged. "If you think there wasn't a thing tonight, then you've got more than your head buried in the sand."

"Maybe you should define it for me," she suggested. It could be something else, although that thought was proof of her attempting to bury her head in said sand.

"Okay." Intensity shone in his eyes. "Tonight at the bar I was having a good time. Things were easy between us. Joking, laughing. Unless I miss my guess, you were enjoying yourself. Or am I wrong?"

She couldn't tell a lie. "You're not wrong."

Some of the tension eased in his jaw and he looked a little surprised. As if he hadn't expected her to admit he was right. "The truth is, I'd very much like to take you out again."

Once more she had to be honest. "I can't do it."

"What? Have fun?"

"I have nothing against fun," she said. "It's going out with you I have a problem with."

"Why?"

"It's not fair to you. I have a child—"

"You can't hide behind Danielle forever." Sloan shook his head and the muscle in his jaw jerked. "Things were fine tonight until you mentioned your husband and real-ized you were having fun. Then it was as if you'd com-mitted an unforgivable sin because for a little while you were a woman who was having a good time with a man and forgot to be a widow."

"You make it sound as if I pull out that designation to wear as a Halloween mask."

"Your words."

"You don't know me well enough to make that call," she accused.

"I'll tell you what I do know." He put his palms flat on the granite island and leaned toward her. "I get that you lost your husband, the man you loved and built a life with. The father of your child. I also admit that I have no idea what you went through. But I do know that it's been several years."

"What does that have to do with anything?"

"I'm getting to that," he said. "The night we kissed, you kissed me back."

"How do you—"

He held up a hand to stop her. "You are forever bring-ing up my reputation with women. Even if only half of the stories are true, it implies that I have a certain level of understanding and familiarity with the fairer sex. I know when there's a spark and when there isn't." His gaze held hers. "You and I could have started a forest fire with all the sparks swirling around us."

Maggie realized he had a point. And she knew her own romantic history could never compete with his in terms of experience. She wasn't good at pretending and wished she could take back that kiss. The fact that he had a point took a lot of the starch out of her comeback choices.

The best she could do was "An out-of-control fire leaves nothing but scorched earth behind."

"That sounds like an Asian proverb and brings me to my point. I do have one," he said. "Either you're still in love with the husband you lost and there's no room in your heart for another man. Or—"

She realized she'd been holding her breath, waiting for him to say the rest. Part of her was afraid to hear the or, but she couldn't stop herself from asking, "Or what?"

"Or you don't believe you deserve to be happy."

That struck a nerve. "Since when does a building contractor dabble in psychobabble?"

"Almost never. But, for some reason, I can't help it with you. So sue me." He dragged his fingers through his hair. "If you're still in love with your husband, that's the end of it. But if you're afraid to be happy, there's something I can do about that."

"Like what?"

Sloan stared at her for several moments without saying anything. Then he just smiled before turning away and walking out of the room.

Maggie had thought there was a lot to think about before. Now her mind was humming with questions about what Sloan planned to do about making her happy.

Chapter Nine

"Sorry I'm late, Maggie." Jill Stone slid into the booth and let out a sigh. The redhead smiled across the table. "Bet you thought I was going to cancel again."

"When one has children, plans are automatically subject to change at a moment's notice. And I was so confident and optimistic that you would be here, I let the hostess seat me." She grinned at her friend. "I'm just glad you made it this time. Let's call it diner lunch, take two."

"Works for me."

"I know C.J. is in school. Where's Sarah? I'm sure you didn't leave her by herself," Maggie said.

Jill laughed at the very idea of it. "My daughter is with her nana and papa. Adam's folks are here from Texas for a visit. They love babysitting."

"Aren't grandparents the best thing ever?" Maggie was lucky to still have her mom. Unfortunately Danny's parents had both passed away even before their son got married. It was sad that Danielle wouldn't have a chance to meet the Potter side of her family. Again there was a stab of guilt over putting off children and the wish that she could change the past.

"The best ever," Jill agreed.

"I guess C.J. is feeling better now?"

Jill shuddered. "It was a nasty virus. Went through the whole family. We ran out of tissues and poor Adam was blowing his nose on toilet paper. At least I never made it here and exposed you. You're lucky."

Maggie's luck was open to interpretation. She'd had lunch with Sloan the day Jill had canceled on her and it had been fun. But he'd also said that her declaration about no more kissing sounded like a challenge. One he'd so far resisted. And the other night he'd implied that he planned to do something to convince her to not be afraid to be happy.

"How's Danielle?" Jill asked.

"Great. Growing too fast. Does it sound horrible if I say that she's the most beautiful, brilliant, sweet, adorable child in the whole world?"

Jill pretended to be shocked. "She can't be. My Sarah is the most stunning, smart, kind—"

"Yeah, yeah." Maggie laughed. "I guess every mom feels that way about her kids."

The server, Brandon Sherman, walked over. "Hi, Maggie. Jill. I see you two made the lunch date work this time. Everyone's okay?"

"My children cooperated by staying healthy," her friend said. "How are you, Brandon? What's going on in your life? Not that we don't enjoy hearing about everything, but it helps us remember what it was like to be young."

"Yeah, you guys are pretty old. Just saying…" He grinned, then said, "I'm great. My online classes are okay. Getting some units out of the way." The teen shrugged. "Just socking away money for school in the fall."

"Where are you planning to go?" Maggie asked. "Somewhere warm?"

"I wish." He grinned. "The University of Montana."

"Do you know what you want to study?" Jill looked at the young man.

"Chemical engineering, I think."

"Wow. Good luck with that," Maggie said. "I guess you're not going to follow your father's footsteps into construction."

Brandon winced. "I have two left thumbs where tools are concerned. And anyway, my dad would be a tough act to follow. He's an artist."

"It's true," Jill chimed in. "When Adam and I had our house built in the Lake Shore subdivision, your dad made the cabinets and they're perfect. He works with Alex McKnight."

"Aren't they involved in the renovations at Blackwater Lake Lodge?" Maggie asked.

"They are," Brandon confirmed. "And with the resort project breaking ground soon, there's some job security for him. Plus, an added financial source for me if necessary."

"You're going places, Brandon. Your parents must be very proud of you." Maggie admired the whole hardworking family.

"Not so much when it comes to cleaning my room or taking out the trash." He grinned and it made him look impossibly young. "I'm glad you guys finally got together for lunch. Although, speaking of that, Maggie did okay when you canceled. She ended up eating with Sloan Holden."

"Oh?" Jill's eyes glittered with the need to know more.

"I'll tell you later." Maggie looked at Brandon. "As you probably already are aware, we don't need menus. I'll have the chicken salad with oil and vinegar dressing. And a diet cola."

"Not me." Jill was looking superior. "I lost weight when I was sick and have room to be bad. I'd like the Mama Bear combo and iced tea."

The teen wrote it on his pad. "Coming right up, ladies."

Maggie watched him walk away. "He's so cute. Someday in the not too distant future he's going to be a heart-breaker."

"You're so right."

"But let's talk about that burger and fries. You're really going to eat it in front of me?" Maggie grumbled.

"Oh, yes. And I plan to savor every bite."

"I may have to steal one, maybe two, of your fries."

"Of course. What are friends for? On one condition," Jill added.

"What?" Here we go, Maggie thought.

"You have to tell me how you ended up with Sloan. What happened?"

"Nothing." Not that day anyway. "When you canceled, I started to leave just as he was coming in. We said hello and the hostess assumed we were two for lunch." She shrugged. "So he insisted we sit at the same table."

"Insisted? You didn't want to?" Jill gave her a "what the heck is wrong with you" look. "I saw him at the chamber of commerce meeting last week. He's gorgeous."

"Looks aren't everything."

"No, but it's not a bad start. And he's renting a room from you. Is he a jerk?"

"Not so far." It would be easier if he were. "He seems like a nice guy. He's not around much, but when he is, Danielle won't leave him alone."

"Oh?"

"On his very first morning at Potter House she was fussy and didn't want either Josie or me. Plus, I was trying to get breakfast on the table." Maggie remembered how he'd jumped in to help. Like a white knight to the rescue. "He made the mistake of taking her outside, which is her favorite place to be. Now he's her hero. The way she acts, you'd think he walks on water."

"So put a check mark in the good-with-kids column."

Clearly Jill was being a loyal friend and wearing her matchmaker's hat.

Still, Maggie was relieved when Brandon arrived with their food, salad for her, burger and fries for Jill. Then he set the drinks in front of them.

"Ketchup is on the table." They gave him a really-this-is-us look and he shrugged. "I know you know, but it's habit. Anything else I can get you?"

"No," they both said.

"Enjoy your lunch."

Maggie knew her friend well and was aware that she would go back to digging for information on Sloan unless she changed the subject. "How are things with you and Adam?"

Jill glowed, and it had nothing to do with her red hair. Quite simply she radiated happiness. "I don't want to say perfect, but it's pretty darn close. Adam is a wonderful man. Handsome, smart, funny, kind. Great with the kids."

"This is coming perilously close to mom bragging," Maggie teased.

"It's different. Trust me."

"How so?"

Jill looked thoughtful, as if trying to find the words to explain. "With kids you love them unconditionally because they come into your life tiny, sweet, innocent. Their future is a blank slate. But when a man becomes part of the equation it's complicated. Everyone comes with flaws and baggage."

"But it's worked out for you." Maggie wasn't asking. She didn't need to. The truth was there on Jill's face, the happiness that made her glow.

"Yes, it worked out pretty darn well." She picked up a fry and bit into it. "We love the new house. It's big and beautiful, but the best part is that Adam has an office right off the family room. I don't mean I like that he has to do paperwork, just that he's home when he does it. Close to the activity."

"Must be nice having him there." Maggie speared some lettuce with her fork.

"It is. He helps C.J. with his homework, and when the weather's nice they play ball outside. My son adores Adam and I'm glad C.J. has a positive role model."

"That's so great."

Smiling, she said, "And he's so sweet with Sarah. He plays with her, whether it's a tea party, dolls or just tickling to make her giggle. That makes us all laugh. It's the cutest thing."

"Children laughing is the sweetest sound."

Maggie felt regret stab her in the heart. Danny never had the chance to see his daughter, let alone play dolls with her or hear her laugh. The sadness that was never far away welled up and stole her appetite. She picked at her salad and sipped her cola. Jill went to town on her burger and ate most of it, but left a few bites.

"I'm so full." She looked across the table and frowned. "Don't you want some of these fries?"

Maggie shook her head. "No, thanks."

"Are you sure?" Jill pushed. "I thought we'd have to arm wrestle for them."

"Actually, I'm not that hungry."

"Is everything all right?" Jill leaned forward a little. "We've been friends for a long time, so I'll know if you're just putting on a brave face."

"Okay, then, I'll come clean." Maggie knew her friend was right and would see through her. "I envy you. I'm not proud of it, and I don't want to say jealous because somehow that sounds resentful and spiteful. So I'll say it this way. I'm envious of the fact that you have such a beautiful family."

"I know you mean it in the nicest possible way and are happy for me," Jill said.

"Absolutely true. You have everything that I ever wanted."

Jill reached over and squeezed her hand. "You can still have it. The right man will come along. Maybe he already has. Sloan seems—"

"No. A person gets one shot at happy-ever-after, and mine died with Danny."

"Maggie, keep an open mind. You just never know what's going to happen."

True. If she had, she would have agreed to have the child her husband had so intensely wanted. Her chest tightened with sadness, regret and a healthy dose of guilt. If he could have known his daughter she might feel differently, but right now she felt that she owed a debt that could never be repaid.

Guilt was turning out to be Maggie's new best friend. It pricked her now because she'd turned this lunch into a slushy, mushy outing and her friend needed lighthearted. Subject change pronto.

"Speaking of not knowing what's going to happen, what can you tell me about the man who bought your old place by the marina on the lake?"

"His name is Jack Garner and he's a writer. His first book was a runaway bestseller. Apparently he's working on the second one and was looking for a quiet place. He liked that mine had an apartment for his office and one for living space. Plus, views of the lake and mountains."

"Did you meet him? How old is he?"

"We did. I'd say he's somewhere in his midthirties. Handsome. Dark. Brooding."

"And reclusive," Maggie said. "As far as I know, no one in town sees him. At least not anyone I know."

"You should go out there, march up to the front door and introduce yourself," Jill suggested.

"Are you playing matchmaker again?"

"What gave me away?" her friend teased.

"Your big, generous heart."

That and the fact that they'd been friends for a long time. Jill had taken shifts at the ice cream parlor when Maggie had experienced a problem in her pregnancy with Danielle and was ordered to stay off her feet. It had made the difference in keeping her business afloat through a very difficult time. And her friend was just interested in helping her now. If only scooping ice cream could fix her current problem.

"I love you for it, Jill." She smiled. "But matchmaking for me is doomed to failure."

"I think your mom is home, Shorty."

Sloan heard a car drive up, but Danielle was completely oblivious. She continued talking to her doll in a language no one but her could understand. It looked as if every toy she owned was on the floor. If there was a way to harness her energy and market it, he could make a fortune. He'd been with her for about an hour and the closest she'd come to stopping was putting her head on his shoulder in a sort of hug. The kid was a hoot and a half.

The front door opened and Maggie walked in carrying a couple of grocery bags. She did a double take, and he figured that had more to do with Josie not being here than the fact that her living room looked as if a toy store exploded inside it.

"Where's Josie?"

Before he could explain, her little girl said, "Mama!"

Maggie smiled. "Hi, baby girl."

The toddler let loose with another stream of unintelligible sounds and an occasional word that was clear. But it was the weirdest thing. The tone, inflection and gesturing looked as if she was explaining that for the past hour he'd been sitting on the floor, playing when encouraged and generally just making sure she was okay.

Maggie set the bags just inside the door and walked over to hug her child. Then she looked down at him and asked again, "Where's Josie?"

"Ah, you don't understand her, either."

"What do you mean?"

"Danielle was just telling you what's going on. It's clearly exposition, but average humans like you and me can't understand."

"Very observant of you, Sloan. But I'd still like to know what's going on. Preferably in exposition that a run-of-the-mill human like myself can comprehend."

"Josie had a date for dinner. The early-bird special, I guess."

"With who?"

A hint of romance brought out the curiosity in a woman, he noted. "She didn't say. It came up suddenly and she was going to call you. I happened to be here working. Mostly to get away from the phone."

"That's what you get for volunteering your number at a town meeting," she pointed out.

"Lesson learned." He watched the little girl tug on her mother's hand, then pat the rug next to him. The message was as clear as Maggie's reluctance to take the hint. Danielle wanted her mother to sit beside him. He was all in favor but Maggie was still waiting for the rest of his explanation. "I told Josie not to bother you to come home early. I needed a break from the work and volunteered to watch Shorty."

"That's very nice of you, Sloan. I hope she hasn't been too much of a bother."

"No trouble at all. I feel like one of those dancers who just stands there while his partner does cartwheels and dances circles around him, making him look like a world-class hoofer." He shrugged. "I just sat here."

"So you were simply keeping her safe."

There was a soft look in Maggie's eyes, the kind of look that made a guy feel like a hero.

"Yeah. I didn't want her to stick her finger in a light socket or invite boys over."

Maggie laughed. "I think that's a few years off. But I can't help wondering what you'd have done if you had to change a diaper. One of *those*."

"One of what?" Then it hit him. "*Oh.* Well… Hmm."

"Yeah. Hmm." She grinned.

"Smart aleck."

"Rookie." She was still smiling. "Have you ever changed a dirty diaper?"

"I've never changed one at all," he said. "But I like to think I'd have rallied to the occasion. Risen to the challenge."

"Oh, how I would have loved to be there for that. I can see the magazine headline now—Dapper Bazillionaire Bachelor on Diaper Duty." This time when her little girl tugged on her hand and patted the rug, Maggie sat beside him. Danielle sat on his thigh, between them.

"I'm sure you would," he said drily.

"Is there anything more irresistible to a woman than a big strong man caring for a child?"

"I don't know. You tell me."

Right here in this house he'd told her that he could do

something about showing her she deserved to be happy and had meant every word. He would bet his last nickel that she hadn't been with anyone since her husband died. That probably should have warned him off, but he couldn't stop himself from wanting her. He wanted to be the man who showed her that life was good and there was nothing wrong with living it to the fullest.

Hell, he wasn't a saint. The fact was, they had chemistry and he couldn't let it go.

"I think one picture of you being nice to a child would have women all over the world throwing themselves at your feet. And breaking into your hotel room."

"Writing their phone number on my cardboard coffee cup?"

"Buying your coffee," she said.

"The thing is, I wasn't asking about whether or not women in general would find me irresistible. I was asking if you do."

A flush crept into her cheeks and she didn't quite meet his gaze. "It doesn't matter what I think."

It did, oddly enough, and the fact that she wouldn't answer directly meant he got the answer he wanted. She might have a problem resisting him. But he sensed that pushing her too far too fast would drive her away.

"Maggie, the truth is that I enjoyed hanging out with your little girl. She's very good company."

"Interesting." She met his gaze now. "Considering the fact that, as you so accurately pointed out, she's not exactly a gifted conversationalist just yet."

"In reality, it was the perfect dialogue. She spilled her secrets in code so I can't rat her out to you. And I ran construction numbers past her while she trashed the room with toys. Everyone is happy." He glanced around and picked up the pink car she'd dropped beside him. "Did you buy her all of these?"

"No way. Most of them came from her uncle."

"Way to go, Brady." Sloan could see himself spoiling a niece or nephew shamelessly.

Then Danielle stood, walked over to a soft stuffed doll and picked it up before wandering around the room with it in her arms as she chattered away.

"Can I ask you a question, Sloan?"

"That was a question."

"You're impossible. I'd hate to be a reporter who was trying to interview you." She made a frustrated sound.

"Okay. Sorry. It's a firmly embedded deflection technique." He'd noticed the tone of her voice had become serious and that made him wonder what she was thinking. If he didn't want to answer, he'd find a way not to. "Ask me anything."

"You're so good with kids." She met his gaze directly and didn't glance away. "Why aren't you married with a family of your own?"

Curious, he thought. It had taken Maggie a while to ask what was usually one of the first things a woman wanted to know about him. Since he was divorced, he would simply tell everyone that he wasn't very good husband material. That had backfired and he was dealing with the consequences and ducking the truth in interviews.

But he didn't want to avoid it with Maggie.

"My mother's Italian. Antonia Delvecchio Holden is outgoing, loving and an incurable romantic."

"She sounds wonderful."

"She is—a force of nature." He couldn't help smiling. "Also pushy, determined and bossy. She believes with every fiber of her being that she knows best. I think it was at my college graduation that she started dropping not-so-subtle hints about me taking a wife and having babies. I just laughed it off, assuming she was joking."

"She wasn't?"

"My mother doesn't joke about that sort of thing," he said ruefully. "The more I ignored her, the more she pressed. Resisting the suggestion of settling down became a reflex for me, automatic."

"But that changed?" Maggie asked.

He nodded. "I met Leigh at a children's hospital charity event. She was a personal trainer. To this day I'm not sure how she scored a ticket to the affair and at the time I really didn't care. I was blown away and thought I'd found *the one.* Just shows how screwed up my judgment is. Then I made the mistake of marrying her first and asking questions later."

"Why?"

Sloan didn't think Maggie was judging him at all, let alone as hard as he was criticizing himself. He remembered his disillusionment and thought about how different his ex-wife was from Maggie. She'd insisted on taking out a small-business loan and turned her home into a B and B to pay for it instead of taking interest-free money from her brother. He looked into her dark brown eyes and knew integrity was staring back at him.

"Shopping and status were more important to my bride than having a family. I ignored the credit card bills coming in, assuming the retail thrill would wear off. But a year later it still hadn't and I thought maybe she needed a different focus." When Maggie opened her mouth to say something, Sloan held up a hand to stop the words. "I know. If the relationship already had problems, bringing a child into it was just going to make it worse. At that point I hadn't admitted it was a mistake."

"What convinced you?"

"I jumped in with both feet and suggested we start a family." A familiar knot of anger and bitterness coiled inside him at the memory. "She laughed and said that it had taken too much work to keep her body in perfect shape. If I wanted her to ruin it, I would have to pay her the big bucks."

"I can't believe anyone would do that." Maggie's eyes grew wide with disbelief. "I assume that before the wedding she understood that you wanted a family."

"Yes. And she claimed to want that, too." He stared at Danielle sitting in the center of the room fitting together plastic blocks that were as big as her tiny hands. This child had been conceived out of love, the way it should be. "She lied to me."

"That's really low." There was sympathy in Maggie's gaze and something else that wasn't as clear.

"I took the failure of my marriage badly, but the breakup hit my mother even harder. She'd grown attached to Leigh and treated her like one of her own daughters."

"That doesn't make you bad husband material," Maggie pointed out.

"It's proof that my judgment is flawed, which is almost the same thing."

"I see. And now you have trust issues."

"Yes." That was part of it. The other part was being made a fool of. Sloan wouldn't let it happen again.

"That's too bad. You'd have made a terrific father."

"Back at you." At her blank look he said, "It's too bad you're standing in your own way, because you're a terrific mom and should have more children."

Her existing child had disappeared from sight and there was a suspicious rustling of bags by the front door.

Maggie didn't seem to hear it. She was looking at him

intently. "Aren't we a pair. Both of us with so much baggage we're tripping over it."

Sloan was almost sure there was regret in her comment, a chink in her armor. Before he could ask, Danielle toddled over to them with a box in her hands.

"Cookie," she said.

Maggie laughed, then looked at Sloan. "What was that you said about not understanding her?"

"I believe I said an occasional word was comprehensible."

"Why did it have to be this one?" She took the box from her daughter, who started to protest loudly. "Just one. You'll spoil your appetite."

Sloan definitely felt regret when she stood and walked away because he missed the warmth of her body and the sweetness of her that was like sunshine to the soul. But he didn't regret answering her question about why he'd vowed never to marry again. He was glad he'd given her the facts. She should know what she was getting into when she slept with him.

And she would. He would bet his last nickel on it.

Chapter Ten

Sloan was having trouble concentrating on work. Maggie was on his mind, more specifically her reaction to learning why he never planned to marry again. The problem was, he'd been unable to gauge her reaction. Would that strengthen her resistance to anything personal between them?

With an effort, he pushed that problem to the side for right now. He and Burke were in his cousin's office with Ellie McKnight, their local architect. She was sitting in the chair behind the desk while they stood on either side of her, going over preliminary plans for the new resort complex near the base of the mountain.

Sloan was intently studying the blueprints and zeroed in on the hotel walls. "You know there's a plastic wrap that can be put around the building to reduce the amount of air leakage through the envelope, that barrier between inside and outside."

"I'm aware of it." Ellie tucked a strand of long brown hair behind her ear then made a note on the plans. "I've included an initial materials list for your consideration, alteration and approval."

Burke nodded absently as he studied the top paper on the thick stack that was nearly as wide as his desk. "At the risk of sending you screaming from the room, Ellie, can we round these walls that face north? It's more self-contained that way. The interior temperature is comfortably maintained without an increase in energy usage."

"I can do anything you want," she said cheerfully. "You've both made it clear that it isn't just the construction process that needs to be green, but the energy sustainability of the building itself."

Sloan was glancing through the list Ellie had provided. "I don't see it on here, but I can provide you the information. There's an innovation for elevators. A company has put a high-friction polyurethane coating over a carbon-fiber core to create a lighter and stronger conventional steel rope. It eliminates the disadvantages of the material currently being used, and the efficiency reduces energy consumption."

"Can you make a note of that on the list?" Ellie asked.

"Of course." He grabbed a pencil from Burke's desk and did as requested.

Sloan knew that the foundation of any construction project was rooted in the concept and design stages. Building, as a process, wasn't streamlined and changed from project to project. Each one was complex, composed of a multitude of materials and components, each constituting various design variables. Any difference in one of them could affect the environment during the building's relevant life cycle. It was important to get this right, and they plowed through the details for the rest of the morning.

"I think we've got this," Sloan finally said, glancing at his watch. Noting that it was just after one, he picked up the phone and asked his assistant to order in some food from the Harvest Café. "I don't know about anyone else but I'm starving."

"Right there with you," Burke said.

"I hope the café sandwiches are all right with you two?"

"I love the food there," Ellie chimed in.

"Me, too." Burke straightened and looked at the architect. "This is really good work."

She flashed a pleased smile and said in her charming Texas drawl, "Aw, you're just sayin' that because you're engaged to my sister-in-law and would rather walk on hot coals than have her mad at you for hurting my feelings."

"No offense," his cousin said, "but this is business and I can't worry about your emotional well-being. That's your husband's job."

"And Alex is really good at it, but you're talkin' awfully brave," she teased. "Seriously, I'm glad you're happy with the overall design. I will incorporate all the changes you've mentioned. And it has to be said that I'm thrilled to have the opportunity to work with your firm. It will be an impressive addition to my résumé."

"You're very talented and we're lucky to have you," Burke said. "And I'm impressed by your conscientious attention to detail, your punctuality and, most important, you really listen."

"Thank you for saying so. My goal is always to be as professional as possible."

"It may not be completely professional, but I believe it falls under the heading of friendliness to ask about someone's family. So I'm going to," Burke said. "You have a little girl, don't you?"

"Yes. Leah."

Sloan had heard about pregnancy glow, but nothing about the glow of pride on a mother's face when talking about her child. Although he'd seen Maggie wear that look every time she glanced at her daughter. "How old is Leah?"

"A little over two. A challenging age for sure."

Right around the same age as Danielle, and he wouldn't

describe her as challenging. Cute as could be, maybe, but not difficult. But he wasn't her primary parent and didn't feel the weight of responsibility for her whole life. If it were up to him, he would give her a cookie whenever she wanted one, so it was probably a good thing it wasn't up to him.

Burke's blue eyes twinkled as he looked down at Ellie. "Syd has promised me that our first child will be a boy, to put a halt to pink domination in the younger generation of her family."

"Don't look now," Ellie said, "but she really has no control over that."

"The truth is that I don't really care about the gender of our children. A little girl as beautiful as her mother would be fine with me."

"That's what I thought. Trust me when I say you weren't fooling anyone." She leaned back in the desk chair and studied his cousin. "But all this talk about children makes me wonder. Is there an imminent announcement on that front?"

"No," Burke said. "We've discussed it, of course. Syd wants to wait awhile. Have some time for just the two of us. And I want what she wants. Making her happy is the most important thing."

"She's a lucky girl," Ellie said. "She's also right. After kids come along everything will be different forever. There's no more being selfish, doing what you want anytime you feel like it. There's another little human whose needs come first." She smiled and her green eyes grew tender. "The weird thing is, you don't really mind. There's an overwhelming compulsion to do anything and everything to make your child's life as perfect as possible."

Sloan listened to his cousin and their architect discuss relationships with present family and future expansions of it. Again he felt as if he was on the outside looking in, a little empty. No personal experiences to share. Well, that wasn't completely true. A time or two he almost jumped in with a comment about Maggie, her daughter and the obvious maternal devotion.

What stopped him was that any interjection would change the dynamic of this conversation and shift attention to him. And Maggie. He would push back and say there was no him and Maggie. Not because he was against the idea. And maybe she was beginning to weaken. Last night, after he made sure she understood that he wasn't a forever-after kind of guy, he'd seen her regret and possibly a decline in her resistance. He couldn't help contemplating his next move and wasn't willing to discuss it.

"Right, Sloan?"

"Hmm?" He heard his name and knew a question was being asked, but had no idea what it was.

"I said, the partial closing of Blackwater Lake Lodge has really affected you."

"Yes. Right."

If he'd been able to get a room there, things would be different. He would probably have met Maggie, but doubted he'd have kissed her in the moonlight. The problem with kissing her was that it made him want more. Living in the same house, looking without touching, was skewering his focus and cranking up a need that grew more intense every day.

"How has it affected you?" Ellie asked. "Good or bad?"

"Both," he answered honestly.

"Specifically?" Burke pushed.

"Home-cooked meals go in the good column. And not living in a hotel for this extended assignment is great."

"What are the negatives?" Ellie wondered.

Maggie. Getting sucked in and captivated by her. Distracted every time he looked at or thought about her mouth, which led to contemplating what she looked like naked. He wasn't going to say any of that, however.

"I don't know. It's just different, I guess."

"Alex is doing the repairs and renovations," Ellie volunteered. "He says it will only be a few more weeks until the cosmetic details are complete. Soon everything will be shiny, new and ready to resume full operations. The rooms are up and running and I know they're taking reservations and accepting guests. And the restaurant is back in business. It's the lobby area and reception/banquet rooms he's concentrating on now."

"So." Burke sat on the corner of the desk. "It should be ready for my engagement party."

"Yes," Ellie answered.

"What party?" Sloan didn't know about this.

"Didn't I tell you?" His cousin frowned. "Damn, I meant to. Syd and I are having a party to celebrate our engagement. Don't you ever talk to your family?"

"Yes." But Sloan realized it had been a while. "Why?"

"I invited your folks and siblings. They would have said something to you if you ever got in touch with them."

"They're not coming, are they?" he teased.

Burke laughed. "Unless they cancel at the last minute, they said to count them in."

"Oh, boy. Do you think Syd is ready for that?"

"She has brothers," the other man said confidently. "She's ready for anything. Besides, you have a terrific family. I spent a lot of time at your house growing up and I know this for a fact."

"I can't wait to meet them," Ellie commented.

"Well, I hope it will be fun for everyone who got an invitation." Sloan folded his arms over his chest.

"Aren't you coming?" his cousin asked.

"I wasn't invited."

"Technically you are. I just forgot to tell you." He shrugged. "I've been busy."

"Yeah, I hear that." Sloan grinned. "Of course I'll be there. You're the brother I never had."

"Good. Feel free to bring a plus one."

Ellie's ears perked up. There was no visual confirmation of that fact, but her next statement proved it. "I heard you've been seeing Maggie."

Sloan only wanted to shoot down that rumor because Maggie was so skittish about dating. But there was visual evidence to back up Ellie's statement because the two of them had been out to dinner with Burke and Syd. Then there had been lunch at the diner and a bite to eat at Bar None after the chamber of commerce meeting. All of the above had been in full view of anyone in Blackwater Lake who cared to spread rumors. And that pretty much encompassed everyone in Blackwater Lake.

As far as Maggie was concerned, *date* was a four-letter word that she adamantly refused to use.

"Are you going out with Maggie?" Burke asked.

"I've been trying. But she doesn't make it easy."

At noon Sloan jumped into his car and headed to Maureen O'Keefe's house. Maggie's mom had called that morning and invited him to lunch at her home. She wouldn't hear of him taking her out, so he was on his way. He'd met her briefly in Brady's office, but today's invitation had initially surprised him. Then he'd figured it out. People were talking about him and Maggie and word had reached her mother.

He turned onto the street where Maggie had lived and drove slowly, checking out her old neighborhood. There were well-maintained yards in front of one- and two-story houses. When the GPS told him he was in front of the right one, he parked in front of it and got out. There was a pine tree in the center of the grass with pansies planted around it. He took the brick walkway leading to the wrap-around porch and front door. Almost immediately after he knocked it was answered.

"Sloan. Hello. Thank you for coming on such short notice."

"Thanks for inviting me. It's nice to see you again, Maureen."

"You, as well." She pulled the door open wider. "Please come in."

He did, then sniffed. "Something smells good."

She smiled a little tensely as she closed the door, then said, "I hope you like quiche."

Because real men eat it. There was a message, and now he knew this meeting was going to be a thing.

"Please come into the kitchen. Can I get you something to drink? Iced tea? Water? Soda? Wine? Beer?"

"I have a busy afternoon, so iced tea would be great."

While she got his drink, Sloan looked around. A granite-topped bar lined with stools separated the kitchen and family room. In it there was a fireplace with a mantel and above it was a flat-screen TV. Wood floors were broken up by area rugs scattered throughout the room. On the walls were beautiful framed pictures of scenes that looked familiar.

Maureen set a tall glass on the bar in front of him. "Here you are."

"Thanks." He glanced around the family room. "Are those pictures on the walls of the mountains and lake here in town?"

"Yes, they are." Her tone indicated surprise and maybe that she was a tiny bit impressed that he'd recognized the subject matter. "They were taken by April Kennedy, a local photographer."

"I've seen her store on Main Street. The composition of the shots is wonderful and the shadows and reflection of mountains on water gives them a black-and-white sort of haunting look."

"Obviously you like them. You should stop by the store and see her. She has a lot more for sale."

"Right now I have nowhere to hang them."

"Because you're staying at my daughter's B and B." Dark eyes—Maggie's eyes—narrowed slightly, indicating a transition into her real reason for inviting him to lunch.

Sloan didn't get to be a successful businessman by dodging the tough issues. And there was no doubt in his mind that Maureen O'Keefe was tough. What surprised him was his unexpected reaction to the third degree he knew was coming. He really cared what Maggie's mom thought of him. Judging by what he knew of her daughter, this woman wouldn't respect anyone who didn't deal with her in a blunt, outspoken and honest way. Fortunately that's the only way he would deal.

"You didn't invite me to lunch just to be neighborly," he said. "This is about Maggie."

"And Danielle." Standing on the other side of the bar, she studied him for a moment, her hands gripping a coffee mug. "My daughter told me about you watching my granddaughter the night before last."

Sloan felt like a sixteen-year-old being interrogated about his intentions. He was so tempted to babble about his motivations being pure to convince her he wasn't a bad guy. But long ago he'd learned it was always best not to embellish. In everything you said there could be something to use against you. So he forced himself to respond only to the question.

"I did."

"You volunteered?"

"Yes."

"Why would you?" The look she gave him said "convince me you're sincere."

"I was just trying to help out. Josie had to leave before Maggie got home from work. I was there doing paperwork and needed a break." He shrugged. "It was a win for everyone."

"And you got to look like a hero." Maureen studied him for any sign that she was right.

"That wasn't my intention. It was knee-jerk. Just responding to the situation in a helpful way." He'd told her the truth; now it was time to push back a little. "Do you have a problem with that?"

"What I have a problem with is a playboy prancing into Maggie's life and sweeping her off her feet."

"Okay. Let's get something straight. I almost never prance."

One corner of Maureen's mouth curved up for a moment, then the humor faded. "But you didn't deny that you're a playboy."

"I am a male. But I don't appreciate being labeled as a man who toys with a woman's emotions."

"There are a lot of stories in newspapers that beg to differ with you about that." She took a sip of coffee. "Seems to me if there wasn't some truth in them, you would be filing lawsuits right and left."

"I have sued when lies were printed that hurt someone's reputation," he said.

"What about yours?"

Sloan could live with it mostly by ignoring what was printed. Number one: getting his name in the paper was a plug for his company. Number two: the sensational nature of the stories actually did him a favor. The women who came on to him because he was a wealthy, eligible bachelor were the ones he had no interest in. To anyone else, the articles were a horrible warning to avoid him like nuclear waste. It saved him from any temptation to break his no-commitment vow.

"My reputation," he said, "is what it is. Anyone I care about who really knows me is aware that's not who I am. The rest—" he shrugged "—I don't really give a rat's behind what they think."

"I guess I fall into the latter category."

"No, that's not what I meant—"

She held up a hand to stop him. "Whether you did or not doesn't change what I have to say. You're a paying customer at my daughter's bed-and-breakfast. I understand that's business. But things seemed to have taken a personal turn when you volunteered to babysit my granddaughter. I feel compelled to protect the two of them and warn you that if you're playing games with their affections it would be a very good idea for you to back off now."

"I assure you that's not what I'm doing."

"Maggie has been hurt enough."

Sloan met her gaze. "I understand what you're saying. I get it."

"Do you?" One of her eyebrows rose questioningly.

"Yes. I can't force you to believe me, but I would never deliberately cause Maggie distress."

"I truly hope you mean that."

"I've never meant anything more in my life. She's a special woman."

Maureen's face softened. "You'll get no argument from me about that."

He ran a finger through the condensation on the outside of his iced-tea glass. "The thing is, Maggie doesn't want another relationship. She's deliberately pushing me away. And before you say anything, I'm almost certain it's not only about losing her husband."

She frowned at him. "Why would you say that? How can you possibly know?"

"I kissed her."

"I know. She told me."

"She did?"

"It was two against one. Josie was on my side. Maggie said the kiss was nothing and both of you realized it meant nothing. Then she told us that you're a womanizer who's not interested in a commitment. That you're a nice man. Good with kids, but all flirt and no depth." Maureen shrugged. "I have perfect recall."

"I can see that." He was impressed. "What she may or may not have told you is that it was kind of her idea. She was going on about outrageous tabloid stories I was featured in and I jokingly asked if there was any way to stop her. She said, and I quote, 'feed me or kiss me.'" He shrugged. "So I did and she kissed me back. It affected her and meant something. But ever since it happened, she's been keeping me at arm's length."

"Maybe you're wrong about the kiss."

"I'm not."

He met her gaze, trying to decide whether or not he should tell her how he could be so sure. Then he realized he had to. This woman cared about her family and wanted to protect them. Sloan wanted that, too, even if it meant doing something to protect her from herself.

"I know she's attracted to me, Maureen. You're probably thinking that's ego talking, but that's not the case. It's experience. I'm not a playboy. I don't lead women on, but I do have a—what should I call it?"

"Active social life?" Maureen suggested wryly.

"That works. The thing is, I've met a lot of women and I can tell when someone is just pretending or when she's sincere. Your daughter doesn't have a dishonest cell in her body. She's open and honest. What she's feeling is right there on her face. Anyone who takes the time to look can see what's inside her." He met her gaze. "Believe me when I tell you that she kissed me back, then retreated from what she was feeling."

"Josie said she didn't believe Maggie when she said it was nothing." Concern replaced distrust on the older woman's face. "It doesn't take a gifted psychologist to realize she was devastated after losing Danny and doesn't want to fall in love and risk being hurt again."

Sloan figured she didn't pretend any more than her daughter did and was starting to believe him. "It feels to me as if she's refusing to let herself be happy. Like a punishment for something."

"What?"

"I wish I knew."

"If you're right," her mom said, "I have no idea why she would do that."

"You know her better than anyone."

"I used to think so, but it seems you know more about her than I do." She smiled, the first genuine warmth she'd exhibited since opening the door. "You're finding out things I didn't even suspect."

"I have a feeling she's buried whatever it is pretty deep. You have no reason to look for it."

"But I'm her mother."

"And she doesn't want to disappoint you," he said, knowing the feeling all too well.

"She never could do that. But I get it." Maureen sighed. "We should eat. You have a busy afternoon and I promised you lunch."

"It smells good," he said again. This time he grinned. "And I happen to like quiche very much."

She looked uncomfortable. "Don't hold it against me. I planned the menu when I was sure you were a heartless jerk."

"I have a heart," he told her. "But there are people who would tell you that there's no question I'm a jerk."

"I'm not one of them." She nodded resolutely. "I'll put the food on the table."

Sloan insisted on helping her. He needed something to keep his hands busy while his mind raced. And he came to a decision.

Since he was the one who'd discovered Maggie wouldn't let herself be happy, it seemed like his responsibility to find out why.

Chapter Eleven

After lunch with Maureen O'Keefe, Sloan returned to work. When he exited the elevator into the reception area on his floor he found Brady O'Keefe waiting for him. And the man didn't look happy.

"You're scowling. Did your computer hard drive crash? Or come up with a particularly nasty virus? Maybe someone didn't pay rent on their office space? I'll check with my assistant about that." Sloan looked at her empty chair. "When she gets back from lunch."

"That's not why I'm here. Can we talk? In your office? Where it's private?"

Sloan glanced around the obviously empty room. "What's wrong with this?"

"Trust me. You're going to want to have this conversation behind closed doors."

This had to be about Maggie. First her mother and now this. Sloan recognized the protective-big-brother look that was all over the other man, from the tension in his body to the hostility in his eyes.

"Okay." He walked into his office and shut the door after the other man followed. It was probably a good idea to put the desk between them, just in case. Sloan moved around it and sat in his chair. "It might save time if you knew that your mother already gave me the 'I'll hurt you if you hurt my daughter' talk."

Brady looked surprised. "When?"

"A little while ago. She invited me over for lunch. It was enlightening."

"So you're going to back off my sister?"

Sloan leaned forward and rested his forearms on the desk. "Again, in the interest of time, you should know that I don't respond well to threats."

Brady's eyes narrowed. "Since we're baring our souls here, you should know that I don't respond well when a publicity-obsessed playboy uses my niece. Clearly stepping in like a conquering hero was your attempt to get on my sister's good side in order to seduce her."

"You couldn't be more wrong."

"So you didn't babysit Danielle until Maggie got home when Josie had to leave?"

"No. I did."

"So you admit you're trying to get my sister in your bed?" Brady braced his feet wide apart and folded his arms over his chest.

Sloan *wanted* Maggie in his bed, but he hadn't watched Danielle to manipulate the situation in his favor. Still, he knew Brady didn't want an answer quite that blunt. Every woman could be a guy's sister, and being protective was just what brothers did. But there was no fighting the chemistry between women and men, and if your sister wanted to sleep with a guy, she would do it whether you approved of her actions or not. Sloan knew about these things.

"I will admit that I like Maggie. A lot," he added emphatically.

"If you like her, then leave her alone."

Sloan blew out a long breath. "Look, I'm not the heartless bastard the tabloids make me out to be."

"What does that mean?"

"It means that I'm photographed with a lot of women and the facts get twisted and embellished to sell magazines. If I'd really been serious about even half the women they say…"

"What?" Brady prodded.

"Let's just say I don't have that much stamina."

"I'm only concerned about one woman. Are you in love with my sister?" Brady moved closer to the desk and settled his palms flat on top of it, his eyes flashing angrily.

"I've never been in love," Sloan answered honestly. "I've never experienced it. I admire and respect Maggie—raising a child and building a business without help."

"No help? What am I? Chopped liver? I built her new website."

"I'm aware that she's got you and Maureen as backup. And Josie is there. Lucy is her partner. But she's a single mother and doing a great job. At the same time, her business is growing. She's an amazing woman. I can tell you without a doubt that I want to get to know her better. I look forward to finding out what makes her tick."

Sloan had never met anyone like her. He'd dated actresses and models who all had "people" to help them. Maggie was a superwoman and made it look easy. He meant every single word he'd just said, and the truth of it was even more clear to him now that her family was on his case to leave her alone.

"Why should I believe you?" Brady demanded.

"I could give you a PowerPoint presentation, but you know as well as I do that talk is cheap." He met the other man's gaze. "But you can take what I'm about to tell you to the bank. I won't say anything to her that I don't mean. I will never make a promise that I don't intend to keep, then walk away. I understand that she has an impressionable child, and whatever affects Maggie impacts her daughter."

"Very true." The other man nodded, then straightened away from the desk. "Danielle is little now, but she'll be affected even more when she gets older."

"I know." The idea of that little girl being used by a guy to get to her mom made Sloan really angry. "Look, Brady, I don't have any clue where this is going with Maggie. Maybe nowhere, because your sister is as stubborn as they come."

"Tell me about it." Brady sat in one of the chairs facing the desk. "I'm the guy she didn't come to for a business loan."

"Maggie has a mind of her own, so your guess is as good as mine about her. Probably better since she's your sister and you grew up with her." Sloan met the other man's gaze. "I can't promise she won't get hurt, but you can count on this. I will never lie to her or treat her with less than the utmost respect."

Brady nodded his understanding, then said, "Damn you."

"Excuse me? Now what's your problem?" Sloan didn't know what else to say. "So you want me to cut my wrist and sign something in blood?"

"As appealing as that sounds…" Brady grinned. "No. I'm ticked off because you were honest."

"What?" Sloan shook his head. "Now you've lost me."

"Okay, then, let me explain. If you were a low-down, lying, cheating, shallow bastard, it would give me an excuse to beat you up."

"Ah. Understood." Sloan smiled slowly. "Well, if it's any consolation, your mother made me eat salad and quiche for lunch."

"Dude—" Brady shook his head sympathetically. "Girl food. That's harsh."

"I'll survive."

"But that's going to leave a scar on your man card."

Sloan shrugged. "Chicks dig scars."

"I've heard that rumor." The other man stood. "I'll have to ask Olivia, my significant other and so much better half, whether or not that's true."

"Let me know the verdict."

"Will do." Brady headed for the door and opened it, then hesitated before leaving. "I hope you're not offended that I interfered. Another guy might—"

"I have three sisters."

"Dude," he said again in that sympathetic tone. "Tell me they're married."

Sloan shook his head. "All single."

"Harsh."

"Well said." He grinned. "And don't worry. We're good. I'd have done the same thing if I were in your shoes."

"Okay. And now I'm going to call my mother and give her a stern lecture about keeping me up-to-date so that I don't pile on when not absolutely necessary."

"Give Maureen my best."

Brady nodded. "Will do."

Alone in his office, Sloan thought about the conversations with Maggie's mother and brother. Commendable loyalty. There was a lot to admire about her whole family. If any of his sisters were in a situation like Maggie's, he would have done exactly what Maureen and Brady O'Keefe had done.

The thing was, he'd meant every single word he'd said to both of them. And that brought him to the law of unintended consequences. They'd forced him to put his intentions into words, made him really think about him and

Maggie and the price of his actions. Not only for him and Maggie, but Danielle, too.

His life would be much less complicated if he'd agreed to back off, but he just couldn't bring himself to do it. He thought about her, dreamed about her, ached to kiss her again and touch her everywhere.

When he gave his word, he kept it and took great pride in that. If he'd promised not to get personal with Maggie, it would have been a lie. Oh, he'd have tried his best, but the forces drawing them together seemed to have other ideas. So he couldn't tell her family that she was off-limits to him.

He really hoped he didn't come to regret that decision.

Maggie had just turned on her office computer and opened a business spreadsheet when she heard her cell phone. It was Josie's ring and she answered.

"Hey, Josie. I just left you. Is my little angel driving you crazy already?"

"I'm so sorry to call, Maggie. But I can't watch her today. There's an emergency. It's Hank Fletcher."

"The sheriff?" This was almost unbelievable; the man was barely sixty and in great physical shape. "What's wrong?"

"He was taken to Mercy Medical Clinic here in town. Adam thinks he had a heart attack."

"Oh, my God."

"He's being taken to the hospital in Copper Hill. I'm going to drive his daughter, Kim, there. She's pretty upset."

Maggie knew the trauma center was an hour away. She was supposed to have given birth to Danielle there but had gone into labor a little earlier than expected and Adam had delivered her. "I can imagine how she feels."

"She called her brother, Will. You remember him, he's

a detective with Chicago PD now." Josie was normally unflappable, but she was rambling and sounded really shaken.

"I've heard about him."

"Anyway, I don't know how long I'll be. They're going to do tests and Kim will need support until her brother can get here."

"Of course she will. I'll come home right now—"

"I can drop Danielle off on my way to pick up Kim. That will be faster."

"If you're sure. That would be great."

"Okay. See you soon."

"Josie, don't worry about this. I'll manage."

"I know you will, sweetheart. 'Bye, Maggie."

"'Bye." She hit the off button and set her phone on the desk.

The spreadsheet on the computer monitor caught her eye and she sighed. There was no point in starting anything because as soon as her daughter got here there would be no work. This whole office would become fodder for exploration. There was nothing Danielle liked more than investigating, aka getting into everything.

Maggie shut off the computer and decided to go down to the café for a cup of coffee. Maybe she could be of help until Josie dropped off Danielle. After taking the rear stairs and walking through the kitchen, she found Lucy circulating around the few tables that were occupied, topping off coffee and making sure no one needed anything.

Her partner saw her and walked over, the empty glass coffeepot in hand. "Hey, I thought you were going to be up to your eyeballs in numbers and budget projections."

"That was the plan. It changed." She looked at Lucy. "Josie called. The sheriff may have had a heart attack. She's going to drive his daughter to the hospital and stay with her."

"Oh, no. I hope he'll be okay." As the situation sank in, Lucy's blue eyes widened. "What are you going to do with Danielle?"

"Good question. I thought I'd have a cup of coffee and contemplate my options while I wait for Josie to drop her off here."

"Have a seat over there by the window," Lucy said. "The breakfast crowd has run its course. Now there are just a few moms who dropped kids at school and came in to eat. They're all taken care of, so I think I'll join you."

"That would be great. An unexpected treat. When life gives you lemons."

"Be right back."

Maggie sat by the window and watched the activity on Main Street. The grocery store was across the way. She'd be willing to bet that after breakfast the moms in here would head over there. Four tables were occupied, two ladies at each of them. She felt a pang of guilt sprinkled with envy about having to work and not be a stay-at-home mom.

The reality was that if Danny had made it back from the war, she would still be a working mom. The difference was that her work time would be more flexible with two people to run the business.

Lucy walked toward her with a steaming mug of coffee in each hand. She put one in front of Maggie then sat across from her. "So this is a good chance to catch up. How are things?"

There was a slight emphasis on the last word, just enough that Maggie knew she wanted to know about Sloan. That was difficult to put into words. The night she'd come home and found him watching Danielle, it was all she could do not to... What? Swoon? Melt into a puddle at his feet? Throw her panties at him?

She didn't know how to reconcile the man who went

through beautiful women like tissues with the one who had volunteered to watch her daughter. She would have thought ten minutes with a toddler would make him curl into the fetal position, but he hadn't done that. He'd actually seemed to enjoy it.

She hadn't known what to make of him and had talked to her mom for the maternal perspective and her brother for the male point of view. Both had said not to worry, but neither knew she *was* teetering on the edge of throwing her panties at him.

She blew on her coffee and finally said, "Things are fine."

"Really? That's all you've got?"

"If you're talking about Sloan, there's really nothing interesting." When did she get to be such a good liar?

"Too bad." Lucy sipped her coffee. "He's got that pretty face, great butt and seems very nice."

He *was* nice, Maggie thought. The other two things were true, too. But between them there were so many reasons not to get involved it was best to ignore all his appealing qualities. It was on the tip of her tongue to suggest again that Lucy chat him up if she had the chance. Again that idea put a knot in her tummy, so she kept her mouth shut.

"So are you seeing anyone?" she asked instead. Best to take the spotlight off herself.

"Oh, no." Lucy seemed more adamant about that than was necessary.

"Wow, that was emphatic." Maggie glanced out the window and saw a Range Rover stop at the curb and park. "Do you want to explain?"

"I know I asked if you'd mind if I flirted with Sloan, but you know better than anyone that I talk the talk but don't walk the walk. And mostly I was testing you out, to see if you were interested. Which, by the way, you are. But suffice it to say, I'm taking a break from men."

"Taking a break or sworn off?"

"Both."

Before she could ask more, Maggie saw Sloan get out of the car that had just pulled up. She'd thought it looked familiar but had been distracted. Her heart stuttered and thumped the way it always did when she saw him, but this time the sighting was unexpected. There hadn't been time to brace herself. He moved to the sidewalk and opened the rear passenger door.

"Speaking of the devil," Lucy said. "There he is now."

"Yeah." Maggie watched him bend over to lean into the backseat.

"Nice butt," her partner observed.

Then he lifted something out of the car and she realized it was a child. Her child.

"What in the world…" She started to get up, but her partner stopped her.

"Wait. Let's see what he does."

"Josie must have asked him to drop her off."

Before she could get up, he walked to the back of the SUV, pressed a button on the key fob and the rear door went up. He pulled out the familiar pink stroller and unfolded it until the thing locked in the open position. He was still holding Danielle when an older couple stopped. Norm and Diane Schurr were regular customers at the ice cream parlor. They stood there for a few moments, smiling and chatting.

Then Sloan started for the café door and Mayor Goodson-McKnight paused beside him to say hello. Danielle had her little arm around his neck and he seemed comfortable, confident and completely unselfconscious.

Maggie noticed that conversation in the café had grown

louder. She caught snippets of "how cute" and "so ador-able." The ladies were smiling as they watched the hand-some man holding her little girl. A chorus of "aw" drifted to her and she understood the sentiment. She felt the same way.

"There's a sight that could almost change a girl's mind about swearing off men." Lucy was practically drooling.

Maggie knew how she felt. That thought pushed her into action and she stood. "I have to go."

"Me, too." Her partner sighed. "When these women in here come to their senses, they're going to want their checks."

Paying a check would be easy compared to Mag-gie's problem. She hurried over to the door just as Sloan was walking inside, pushing the empty stroller. Danielle seemed very comfortable in his arms.

She spotted Maggie and held out her arms. "Mama!"

"Hey, baby girl." Maggie took her and hugged her close for a moment, breathing in the sweet, little-girl scent of her. "Did you go for a ride?"

"Car," she said, pointing to the one at the curb. "Go bye-bye."

"Yes, you did." She looked at Sloan. "I guess Josie asked you to bring her?"

"I volunteered," he said. "I overheard her telling you about what happened to the sheriff and I could see she was in a hurry to get on the road."

"Yeah, I got that feeling, too."

"So here's Danielle," he said. "What are you going to do with her?"

"Call Grandma."

"Gamma?" the toddler said.

"Yes, love. Thank you for bringing her here, Sloan. Hopefully, Grandma is free today." She looked at the man in front of her, whose reputation was completely at odds with his behavior. "And don't worry. I won't tell her about your good deed."

"So you know she talked to me?"

"Yeah, about your ulterior motive in looking after Danielle."

"She invited me to lunch at her house to chat." There was a twinkle in his eyes.

"Sloan, I'm so sorry. She shouldn't have done that."

"It gets better," he said.

His expression was wry and she got it right away. "Brady, too?"

"Man to man," he confirmed.

"That, I didn't know about. Tell me he didn't hit you," she said, a little horrified.

"I was more concerned about him hacking into the company computers and giving us a virus that would wipe out everything. But we talked it through."

"Hugged it out?" she asked.

"And sang, 'Kumbaya,'" he teased.

"Seriously, Sloan, I'm so embarrassed. It never occurred to me that they would interfere and bother you."

"No bother." He smiled at the child in her arms, squirming to get down. "They're concerned about you. I respect that."

"There's concern and then there's meddling. I'll talk to them. Make sure they don't bother you again."

"It's no bother, Maggie. Forget about it."

"As if that's going to happen." She set Danielle on the floor but held on to her. The little girl was pulling against the grip, practically quivering to get into trouble. "I apologize again. And thanks for dropping her off."

"I was coming into town anyway. Maybe the spirit of

this town and helping your neighbors is rubbing off on me." He shrugged. "Now I have to get to work."

"Right." There was a frustrated wail from her daughter, who was still desperately trying to get away. "And I have to see if Mom can watch her."

"I'll see you for dinner?"

"You will. It's chicken piccata night."

"My favorite. Later, then." He looked at her and, just before he walked out the door, something smoldered in his eyes. Something that had her quivering from head to toe, some parts more than others.

Maggie felt the quivers give way to goose bumps as she watched him through the window. She wasn't sure if the neighborliness of this town was rubbing off on him, but he was certainly rubbing off on her.

She felt cracks in her resistance to him and was fairly certain that surrender couldn't be far behind.

Chapter Twelve

"So the sheriff is holding his own?" With the phone to her ear, Maggie leaned back against the kitchen island and waited for Josie to answer.

"They did tests and he's resting comfortably. Doctors will talk to him tomorrow about the results. Will Fletcher is flying in from Chicago," her friend said. "But he can't get here until morning. So I'm going to stay with Kim until then."

"How's her son?" Maggie knew Tim was fourteen and probably worried about his grandfather.

"He's staying with a friend because he's in school. But she calls him or texts all the time. So he's hanging in there."

"Good." Maggie knew that was the best thing. "And thanks for letting me know you won't be back tonight. I would worry."

"You're sweet. I'm so sorry about not being able to watch Danielle. Did it mess you up a lot?"

Only where Sloan was concerned. Seeing him effortlessly handling her daughter had flipped a switch inside her. She glanced at him carrying dishes into the kitchen from the dining room.

Grandma had not been free today, which meant Danielle had hung out in her office. Dinner had been later than usual tonight because the work schedule had fallen apart. It had just been her and Sloan, what with Josie at the hospital and Danielle in bed early for lack of a nap. Now Sloan was helping with dishes instead of leaving it to her like any respectable paying guest would.

How was a girl supposed to resist that?

"Maggie?"

"I'm here." Although her mind was on how sexy Sloan looked in his worn jeans.

"Good, I thought I'd lost you," Josie said. "Did everything work out all right with Danielle?"

"It's fine." That was one good thing about being your own boss. Things worked out; it just took a little longer sometimes than others. "Don't worry about us. Just concentrate on Kim, and if she needs anything let me know. Give her hugs from us."

"Will do. Talk to you tomorrow. 'Bye, Maggie."

"'Bye." The phone went dead and she set it back on the charger.

"What's up?" Sloan set glasses in the sink then met her gaze.

"Hank Fletcher is stable. In the morning the doctors are going to give him test results. There will be more news then."

He nodded and went back to the dining room, returning with leftovers. "So right now it's no news is good news."

"Yes." She stared at him displaying his domestic side. "If I didn't know better, I'd say you're getting ready to do the dishes."

"Look at you. Miss Observant." He grinned. "Not just another pretty face."

The compliment, teasing though it was, warmed a cold,

dark place inside her that hadn't been touched in a long time. She didn't have the energy or will to seal it off now.

"You do know that being charming doesn't mean you get to have your way here in my kitchen."

"Okay." He nodded thoughtfully, but his eyes were twinkling. "Then, let's just go with the fact that hospitality is your goal and it would be hospitable to just give in and let me help."

"I can't talk you out of this, can I?"

"No."

"Then, let's go with hospitality." *Be still my heart*, she thought. "I'll put the food away."

"Teamwork," he said. "I like it."

And she liked him. So much more than she wanted to. Maggie's hands were busy and so was her mind. As she put leftover chicken, mashed potatoes and green beans into containers, she was trying to figure out Sloan Holden's deal. He must have a flaw. Everyone did. No one was this nice, this perfect.

More than that, no man that nice and so nearly perfect should still be an eligible bachelor. Except he'd told her why he would never get married again. So she was pretty far gone that even his honesty was sexy to her. How could she not admire that he'd put his cards on the table and let a woman decide whether or not to play when she knew what the game was?

So far, Maggie had resisted him, but the longer they were alone, the more she believed *him* being alone was somehow wrong.

"It's been one of those days for you," he said when the kitchen chores were finished. "What do you think about you and I having a glass of wine?"

Her head was warning danger, but her hormones were telling her head to shut the heck up.

The hormones won. "Great ideas like that are responsible for your business success."

"Nice to be appreciated. And I have another world-class suggestion."

"What would that be?" she asked.

"We should turn on the gas log in the fireplace and have our wine in the great room." Flecks of gold in his brown eyes glowed with a hint of challenge.

God help her, that dare sounded wonderful and she couldn't walk away from it tonight. "Another great idea."

Look at her—all grown-up and sophisticated. No nerves in her voice, at least none that she could detect. This was just too much temptation to defend against. Talking with a handsome man in front of a fire. There was no harm in that, right?

She retrieved a bottle of cabernet from the center island's built-in wine rack, then Sloan expertly opened it with the corkscrew she handed him. After she pulled two stemmed glasses from the china hutch in the dining room, he poured and then held one out to her.

"Let's go sit." She turned off all but the beneath-the-cabinet lights to dim the brightness.

He followed her into the other room. Beside the river-rock fireplace was a switch, and when she flipped it, flames instantly danced around the gas log, which was behind glass doors.

Sloan waited until she sat on the sofa, then lowered himself beside her, not too close, but close enough to touch her without moving.

Maggie was suddenly nervous and took a sip of wine. "This is—nice."

"Out of all possible words to use, *nice* is the best you could come up with?"

"Do we need to have another stern talk about your ego, Mr. Holden?"

He laughed. "With you there's never a risk of it getting out of control. I was just hoping for a little more detail about what you're feeling."

"Okay." She took another sip of the deep red liquid. "I can't remember the last time I had a relaxing evening stretching in front of me. Usually it's bath time, then a battle to convince a reluctant toddler she should get some sleep."

"It's a lot of work." He drank his wine and watched her.

"That's an understatement." Maggie would never be sure why the next words came out of her mouth, but once said there was no putting them back. "Danny wanted children right away. He said it would make him the happiest man on earth if I got pregnant on our honeymoon."

"But you didn't agree." He shrugged as if to say it was a no-brainer. "You said he wanted it. Not that the two of you did."

"You're observant, too." Maggie met his gaze. Flames reflected in the green flecks in his brown eyes, but there was no judgment in his expression. "I wanted to wait. We had a lot going on with getting the ice cream parlor opened. And I just wanted time for the two of us alone."

"That's understandable. A child changes everything forever." He half turned toward her, his long legs just inches away now. "It's practical. Syd and Burke are waiting."

"And you know all this how?" She sipped from her glass.

"There was a meeting about the resort hotel plans in Burke's office not long ago and Ellie McKnight was there. The subject just came up."

That made her smile. "Is having children a normal topic of conversation during a meeting about blueprints?"

He shook his head and managed to look only a little sheepish. "It's what I like to call the Blackwater Lake Effect."

"What's that?"

"There's something about this town. Some enchanted thing that makes you break the rules of business that would apply anywhere else. And somehow it works."

"Well said." She finished her wine and set the empty glass on the coffee table. "Danny and I agreed on pretty much everything but having a baby right away. We hardly ever fought, but we did about that. Before the wedding we were in agreement on having kids but never talked about the time frame for doing it."

"Do you know why he felt that way?"

"He didn't say, but my theory is that he had a feeling he was going to die."

"He was in the military and knew he could deploy to a war zone. It makes sense that he would think about the possibility."

"I didn't. I wouldn't ever consider that he might not come home to me." She felt the familiar self-blame welling up inside her. "He really loved kids and wanted to see his child before he had to leave." There was a catch in her voice and she swallowed. "But he never did."

"And you feel guilty about it."

"Of course. Because I was selfish, he never had a chance to see his daughter."

"So that's what you've been carrying around," he said.

"Pretty much. How can I not?"

"Maggie…" His tone was scolding and sympathetic at the same time. Sloan set his glass on the table beside hers, then moved close and cupped her face in his hands. "Don't do this to yourself."

"I did it to him. Don't you see?"

"It's not your fault," he said gently. "A person can't really be true to herself if she's making decisions based on the fact that her partner might not be around tomorrow. Sure, it's a variable you factor in because of his military service, but you have nothing to feel guilty about. It's stopping you from being happy."

"How can I? I'm here and he's not."

"By all accounts, your husband was a good guy. He would want you to go on living. Have a full and satisfying life."

Danny had said as much to her, but she was curious about Sloan's perspective. "How can you be so sure?"

"Because if I loved someone and couldn't be there for them, I wouldn't want that person to be lonely and unhappy. I think Danny would feel the same."

Having another man's point of view seemed to validate what her husband had said, and the words struck a chord with her. Either they were exactly the right thing to say, or maybe she was just ready to hear them. Either way, Maggie felt something inside her shift and a great weight lifted from her heart.

"Danny *was* a good guy," she said softly.

"Of course he was." His voice was emphatic. "You wouldn't have chosen him if he wasn't."

"That's very nice of you to say." Maggie looked into his eyes and saw something smoldering there, something sizzling and incredibly exciting. "Are you going to kiss me?"

"You have no idea how badly I want to."

"I'd like that very much."

"Are you sure?" His gaze searched hers.

"Yes."

She'd barely spoken when he claimed her mouth. It was like touching a match to dry grass, and heat exploded inside her. He pulled her onto his lap and settled a big hand at her waist. While their mouths teased and taunted, his thumb brushed over her midriff and grazed the underside of her breast. The touch, so tentative and tantalizing, made her want more.

She linked her arms around his neck and pressed her breasts to his chest. There was a hitch in his breathing and it grew ragged. He folded her in his strong arms and held her tight. Sliding his fingers into her hair, he gently cupped the back of her head to make the contact of their mouths more firm.

When he traced her bottom lip with his tongue, she opened her mouth, inviting him inside. Without hesitation he entered and explored, caressed and coaxed. She felt there was a very real promise of going up in flames, and was so ready for that to happen.

Sloan pulled back, his mouth an inch from hers. He was breathing hard, but managed to say, "What are the chances of getting an invitation into your bedroom to see if the faucet is okay?"

She knew he was referring to her warning not to expect to be invited. Now he knew it had been an empty threat. "The plumber has been here, so I'm sure it's fine."

"It could still be leaking."

"I'm not worried about it." Then she grinned. "But if you'd like to come into my bedroom and check out the thread count of my sheets, that would be all right with me."

"Just all right?" His gaze was hooded, smoky, sexy.

"More than all right—"

"If you're sure…"

"Absolutely." She slid off his lap and took his hand in hers. "I really want you to see my bedroom."

"So this is all about me?"

"Yes."

He stood and smiled like a man who'd just gotten everything he wanted for Christmas. "That works for me."

Hand in hand they walked through the house to the double-door entry of her room. She turned on the hall light and glanced at the room across from them, where Danielle was soundly sleeping in her crib.

Maggie opened her bedroom door, revealing the king-size bed with the wedding ring–patterned spread and a lot of pink-and-green throw pillows. In the far shadows there was an oak dresser and matching armoire. A glider chair, which she'd almost worn out when her daughter was a newborn, sat in the corner. A right-hand turn led to the master bath with its two sinks.

"Maggie?" There was concern on his face and it was incredibly sweet.

She felt Sloan's hesitation and looked up. "I'm okay."

"Are you really sure about this?"

"Yes."

He nodded. "Then, while you turn down the bed, I need to go upstairs and get something."

With that, he turned and hurried back the way he'd come. What in the world? She hadn't done this for a long time, but it didn't sound as if he'd changed his mind. Even if he had, the bed still needed to be undressed. As she stowed the throw pillows on the glider chair and rolled the spread to the end of the bed, she thought about that word. *Undressed.*

The bed wasn't all that needed undressing. She would have to take off her clothes. And get naked.

Just then a large shape filled the doorway. It was obvious because the light was cut off. "I'm back."

"Okay."

Sloan walked to the nightstand and set a small packet there. A condom. Maybe more. But of course. How could she have forgotten? They would need that after getting naked. He no doubt looked like a Greek god. But she… *Eek!*

"Maggie?" He walked over to her and cupped her face in his hands then tenderly touched his mouth to hers. Pulling away slightly, he said, "What's wrong?"

"Nothing." She was facing the hall and her features were illuminated, showing him what she knew was probably an anxious expression.

"Don't do that." He was in shadow but there was pleading in his tone. "Don't shut me out. Talk to me."

"You'll think I'm crazy. Or worse."

"There's something worse?" He tilted up her face and was obviously studying her. "Tell me what's going on in that mind of yours."

"It's silly. Unimportant. It's—"

He touched a finger to her lips. "I'm not giving up, so you might as well get it over with."

"Okay. It's— I—" She sighed and looked away. "It's been a long time for me. Sex, I mean."

"I knew that."

"I've had a baby."

"Yeah. I met her. Cute kid," he said.

"The thing is, you're a man—"

"Actually, I knew that, too." There was a smile in his tone.

"Now you're laughing at me. Forget it." This was so humiliating. She started to walk past him, but he gently took her arm to stop her.

"I think your cute daughter has a very cute mom. I'm not laughing, Maggie. I'm listening."

She blew out a breath. "Here's the deal. I have stretch marks. My tummy isn't flat. These are childbearing hips."

"If you're trying to turn me on, it's working." His voice was low, uneven, rough.

"You don't get it, so let me spell this out. I'm saying you shouldn't have high expectations, because I'm not like the perfect women you date. You should prepare yourself for a big disappointment."

"Maggie…" He reached out a finger and touched her collarbone then lightly dragged the touch over her chest to her breast. He stopped at her waist and undid the button on her jeans. "There's no way you're talking me out of this."

"I'm only being honest—"

He kissed her, then whispered against her mouth, "Stop talking. More important, stop thinking. You are a beautiful woman. So hot. I've wanted you since the first time I saw you."

"Wow." Her heart pounded. "You can keep talking."

"Actions speak louder." His tone was full of the need to possess and a whole lot of pent-up passion.

Then he kissed her again and she kissed him back. Flames licked through her, setting her on fire with the need to touch his skin. She tugged his cotton shirt from the waistband of his jeans and started undoing the buttons, but her hands were shaking. He brushed them aside and impatiently yanked the thing over his head.

She settled her hands on his chest, one over his hammering heart. The light dusting of hair tickled her palms and made her savor his masculinity. Her breath caught and yearning welled up inside her. It had been so damn long since a man had held her, told her she was beautiful and wanted her.

Sloan pulled off her T-shirt, then unhooked her bra and slid it off. After that, he lowered the zipper on her jeans. In moments she was naked, and held her breath. Instinctively she crossed her arms over her breasts, but he shook his head and gently pulled them away.

"Beautiful," he breathed.

She put her back to the lit hall in order to see his expression. It was everything she could have hoped for and more. "You have to say that."

"No. I don't have to say anything." He shook his head. "I'll tell you a secret. Remember that presentation I did at the chamber of commerce meeting about green building? You were sitting in the third row and seriously messing with my concentration."

"How?" She ran a finger over his chest and grazed a nipple, then smiled when he groaned.

"I kept picturing you like this. And you are even more beautiful than I imagined."

Maggie knew he had a lot of experience to fuel his imagination and if he was lying she didn't care. The compliment did a lot to shore up her female confidence and her shattered soul. "And you, sir, have too many clothes on."

That was all it took for him to set a record for getting out of them. Maggie looked at him the way he'd looked at her. "Better than I imagined, too."

"You thought about me in the altogether? Ms. Potter, I'm shocked."

"Oh, please…"

"Please what?"

She saw the need in his eyes and knew it was a match for her own. "Please take me to bed."

And he did just that, then pulled her against him. They were on their sides facing each other and he ran his palm over the dip at her waist and down her thigh. It felt like magic and moonlight. But he didn't stop there. His fingers brushed her inner thigh and strayed between her legs. She couldn't stop the moan of delight, and unconsciously opened to his exploration. He touched the sensitive bundle of nerves at the heart of her femininity and she nearly shot off the bed from the electric pleasure of it.

"Sloan—" She could hardly talk, her breathing was so uneven. "I want you. Sloan—"

"I know, sweetheart." He was already reaching for the condom and tore open the package. In seconds he had it on, then covered her body with his own.

Slowly he entered her and let her get used to the feel of him. Impatient, Maggie instinctively tilted her hips up, signaling what she wanted. He obliged, pushing into her, moving in and out, taking her higher and higher until sensation blasted through her and shock waves claimed her body.

He held her, stroked her hair until she stilled. Then he moved inside her again. Several moments later he groaned and went still, burying his face where her neck and shoulder met. It was her turn to hold him and she did, loving the way he felt in her arms. They stayed that way for a long time.

Finally he said, "I don't want to move, ever, but I'm afraid I'm crushing you."

"I don't mind." She liked holding him.

But he rolled away and smiled down at her. "In case you were wondering, I am in no way disappointed." He cupped her cheek in his hand and kissed her. "That was perfect."

Maggie appreciated the words. What she didn't appreciate was the way reality had a way of creeping in and obliterating the glow. Sex had been fantastic and he was even more wonderful than she'd thought. She hadn't realized how much she'd missed this intimacy.

But none of that changed her situation. She was still a single mom with a daughter to raise.

After Sloan came back to bed, he pulled her into his arms and they dozed for a little while. Then Maggie rolled away and said she had to check on Danielle. He waited for her to return to him, but she didn't and he knew something was up. Most likely she was thinking too much again. It was time to put a stop to that.

He got up and quickly dressed before going in search of her. He found her on the couch in front of the fire where she'd told him about the guilt she'd carried since her husband died.

He sat down beside her and knew there was nothing on under her navy blue terry-cloth robe. Pushing aside the fact that he wanted her again, just as much as he had earlier, he asked, "Is Danielle okay?"

"Sleeping like a baby." There was a tender smile curving up those full lips. "This probably isn't the best time to tell you, although we used protection, but my little girl is here because of an oops."

"Oh?"

"I was busy, tired, stressed what with getting the business up and running. I forgot that I had to see the doctor to renew my birth control prescription and didn't have time to go. Before you ask, Danny knew and we were careful." She shrugged. "But one night we got carried away. I have to say—best mistake ever."

"If only we could say that about all mistakes," he said.

"She's what got me through the worst time in my life, right after Danny died. I had to take care of myself, not for me but for the baby Danny wanted so much. She's the only part of him that I have left. Then she was born and I fell in love with her. I had to get out of bed whether I wanted to or not."

"I can see how that would be the case." Sloan sensed that she wasn't saying this because he'd asked about her little girl. Maggie had a point and he wanted to know what it was. "What are you trying to tell me?"

"I didn't plan to sleep with you, Sloan. But it happened. And it was wonderful."

If he had to guess, he'd say she didn't want to admit that. Points to her for honesty. It was refreshing. "I hear a *but* coming."

"No." Her lips curved up, but there was the same sadness in her eyes that had been there when they first met, when she'd looked at a picture of her husband. "I just want to clarify. And make sure you don't have an expectation of anything permanent. I mean, you've told me you don't, but that was before we…"

"Slept together," he finished.

"Yes. I wouldn't want you to think I'm leading you on."

"Hey, that's my line." And Sloan was annoyed that she'd stolen it from him.

"So you understand where I'm coming from."

"Yes." But that didn't mean he liked it.

"Good. I'm glad we cleared that up."

It was clear to Sloan that even confessing her secret hadn't eased the guilt she felt. She was holding her emotions close, and he wasn't happy about the distance she'd put between them. That declaration of not wanting to lead him on was particularly annoying because it was the way he'd acted ever since his divorce. How disconcerting to realize that taking Maggie to bed was more than just for fun. It meant something.

He wasn't at all sure how he felt about that. But she was waiting for a response. "I appreciate the warning. It's always good to have things spelled out. What do you say we take things one day at a time?"

"Sounds sensible to me."

For the first time in his life, sensible was about as appealing as banging his head against the wall.

Chapter Thirteen

"It's really above and beyond the call of duty for you to do this," Sloan said.

This being to have his family over for dinner tonight, Maggie thought. He was trying to help her in the kitchen and Danielle was clinging to her leg. Josie was staying in Copper Hill near Hank Fletcher and his family after his heart-bypass surgery a week ago. And in a little while there would be five extra people around her dining room table.

"Not a duty. It's the Blackwater Lake Effect." She shrugged. "We're neighborly."

"Still, you didn't have to and I really appreciate it."

The Holdens were due in about thirty minutes, and as the time ticked by, Maggie wondered if she was a glutton for punishment. Just plain crazy. Or both. Feeding her paying guests was her responsibility, and that didn't technically extend to their relatives.

But she knew they'd been in town for several days, having come early to visit with their son before their nephew's engagement party. Technically they were Burke and Sydney's responsibility. They were staying at the newly renovated Blackwater Lake Lodge, and Sloan had had dinner with them a couple of nights ago at Fireside, the five-star on-site restaurant.

At breakfast the next morning he'd casually mentioned his folks would like to see where he was staying. Maggie was afraid sleeping with Sloan had fueled her curiosity about his family. It didn't matter that she'd agreed with him about not getting serious; she was still curious about his parents and sisters. Whatever the reason, she'd suggested he invite them to dinner and now she was a little intimidated and a lot nervous because they'd accepted. This reaction proved that their positive opinion mattered to her no matter how much she tried to convince herself it didn't.

She'd made most of the simple meal ahead of time, planning to serve roast, mashed potatoes, rolls and broccoli salad, a yummy recipe with onion, raisins and fabulous dressing. Most people were either firmly in the pro or con column on broccoli, but not even one hater had ever complained about her dish. The meat was done and wrapped in aluminum foil to stay warm. Gravy was made and the potatoes needed a final warming up in the microwave. There was only one more thing to do.

Maggie picked up her child. "I have to make biscuits, sweetie, and I can't do that with you glued to my thigh."

The little girl smiled and clapped her hands. "Cookie?"

"How do you always know when to push your advantage?" She sighed, but couldn't help smiling and kissing that precious face.

"What can I do to help?" Sloan asked.

"If you can mix up dough, roll it out and cut circles out of it to put on a baking sheet and into the oven, that would be pretty awesome."

"Sorry," he said. "That's above my pay grade."

"Too bad." She tried to set the little girl on her feet but the toddler pulled her legs up and refused to be put down. "What we have here is a standoff."

"Maybe she'll come to me. We can play with the toys." He held out his arms and Danielle eagerly went into them.

"Dolly?" she asked.

"Let's go find her." He grinned. "And just like that, tensions are resolved."

"Thank you," she said gratefully.

Maggie was mesmerized by the sight of his broad back before he left the room. The memory of being in his arms was never far from her mind, especially at night in her big bed all alone. She knew if he kissed her again it would happen again. But the thought of giving in again gave her pause. Once wasn't serious; twice was a pattern.

The problem was, he'd awakened the need in her that she'd so carefully folded up and put away when her husband died. Even if Sloan changed his mind about taking a chance on a relationship, she couldn't risk it. Raising her daughter the way Danny would have wanted was her job and hers alone.

It only took her about ten minutes to whip up the made-from-scratch rolls, and she put the cookie sheet in the oven. She could keep them warm and fresh, but baking them at the last minute with the distraction of total strangers could be a recipe for disaster.

When the timer dinged, she removed them and placed the steaming rolls in a cloth-lined basket on the stove. She was as ready as possible, and as if that was the cue, the doorbell sounded. Perfect so far, she thought.

She went to greet the newcomers and saw Sloan headed for the door, Danielle hot on his heels. When the little girl stopped and grabbed his leg, the trusting gesture tugged at Maggie's heart. Then he opened the door and chaos erupted when his family walked in.

"Hi, Mom." He hugged the older woman who had

dark hair and eyes. Then he held out his hand to the distinguished-looking, blue-eyed man. "Dad."

"Son." His hair was the same color as Sloan's but shot through with silver.

Three young women who looked to be in their twenties followed the older couple inside and Sloan hugged each one before closing the door. "Mom, Dad, I'd like you to meet Maggie Potter, my landlady." He looked at her, then his parents. "Maggie, this is my mother, Antonia, and my father, Campbell."

She smiled and shook hands with each of them. "It's a pleasure to meet you both."

"Likewise." His mother sized her up. "And please call me Annie. Everyone does."

"Not everyone. We call you Mom," one of his sisters said.

Sloan held out his hand, indicating the young women. "And these three smart alecks are the curse of my existence. My sisters—Carla, Gina and Isabella."

Maggie shook their hands and made mental notes to remember who was who. Carla had dark hair and blue eyes. Gina was a green-eyed redhead. Blonde Isabella's eyes were brown like Sloan's and her mother's.

Danielle had backed away from the invasion of Holdens, looking decidedly uncertain about this turn of events. Now she moved forward and grabbed Sloan's leg again. He picked her up as if the movement was automatic.

"And who's this little angel?" Annie asked.

"Maggie's daughter, Danielle." The look Sloan sent her said he'd clued them in about her being a single mom and why.

"She's gorgeous." Annie glanced at Maggie. "Like her mother."

"She is beautiful," Maggie answered, making this all about her little girl. "But I'm definitely prejudiced."

"Can I get everyone something to drink?" Sloan asked his family.

He'd told her not to worry about that part of the evening's hospitality, that he would handle it. Now she realized how much of the stress it took off her. On the other hand, it added a different kind. This felt so much like being a couple. They weren't, but a pleasurable sensation moved and stretched a little painfully inside her, like muscles that hadn't been used in a long time.

Before filling drink orders, Sloan gave them a tour of the house. Afterward, they all gathered around the kitchen island while he poured a scotch for his father and himself. The women, including Maggie, had wine. Then he handed Danielle a sippy cup with watered-down apple juice. How sweet and thoughtful to make sure she wasn't left out.

"What should we drink to?" Campbell asked.

"To Maggie," his wife said. "And giving our son a home away from home."

Before she could protest that this was part of her business, they were all saying, "To Maggie."

"You're very sweet," she said. "But Sloan is a paying guest and hospitality is my job."

"It's not your job to put up with his family," Annie said. "Thank you for your warmth, kindness and generosity. I think I speak for all of us when I say that."

"You don't speak for me, Mom," Isabella said. "Personally I think Maggie needs to have her head examined for letting my brother stay here. He's a pain in the neck." The young woman was clearly teasing.

"Hey," he protested.

"Izzy, you always were the most headstrong child," her mother scolded.

"Ignore my sister," Sloan advised.

"She's right, though. What if we were horrible to you?" Gina asked.

"There's no what-if about it," Sloan shot back. "You *are* horrible. I warned her but she refused to listen."

"You did not," Maggie said. "What he actually told me was that if anyone got out of line he would take care of them the Chicago way. Do you have any idea what that means?" she teased.

"Not specifically." Campbell's blue eyes twinkled. "But I understand it's not pretty. So you girls better behave yourselves."

"Us?" The three of them spoke together, innocent and outraged at the same time.

"You realize that's sexist, right, Dad?" Carla asked. "What about Sloan? And you?"

Her dad shrugged. "It's four against two. That means the odds favor one of you ladies messing up. And I'm too charming for that."

"No one is going to be mean because they answer to me," Annie assured her. "Do you think Danielle would come to me?"

Maggie studied her daughter, in Sloan's arms because he'd picked her up again. The little girl looked comfortable and Maggie thought if it was her, she wouldn't willingly leave the safety he offered. But that wasn't the question.

"You've raised four children and I don't have to tell you how unpredictable they can be. Give it a try. But please don't be offended if she's shy."

"You're right about unpredictable. Raising these troublemakers prepared me for anything." The older woman walked over to her son and held out her arms to the little girl. She went willingly and Annie cuddled her close. "You are a sweet girl."

"Sometimes yes, sometimes no," Maggie qualified. "But my mother would tell you that she's always perfect."

"Your mother is very fortunate to have a grandchild." She gave her four children a look. "I'm still waiting."

Sloan cleared his throat. "I think it's time for dinner, don't you, Maggie?"

She wanted to laugh but didn't. He so clearly wanted a distraction. "Everything is ready. If you'll all have a seat in the dining room, I'll put the food out."

"I'll help." Sloan's expression pleaded to be kept busy.

"That would be great," she said. "You can settle Danielle in her high chair."

"Remind me to ask about you knowing how to do that," Annie said. "But would you mind if I put her in?"

"That would be great. Thanks."

Maggie found herself liking these people a lot. Meeting them explained how Sloan was so down-to-earth in spite of all his money and the playboy reputation. This family would never let him get too full of himself. It would be so much easier if she found him annoyingly pompous and egotistical.

Dinner went better than she'd hoped, and it seemed everyone was having a good time. When they finished eating, Sloan and his mother offered to help her clean up and wouldn't take no for an answer. They were rinsing off dishes while the other Holdens played with Danielle.

"It's so nice that you didn't have to stay in a hotel while working on the resort," his mother said.

Sloan was looking at Maggie when he answered, "There's definitely an upside."

Annie glanced between them, a pleased look shining in her eyes. "You're a lucky man. Finding someone as pretty and wholesome as Maggie is a plus."

"You mean, finding my bed-and-breakfast," Maggie clarified.

Dishcloth in hand, Annie stood with her back to the sink. "No, I meant *you*. I like you very much."

"That's awfully nice of you to say." Maggie recalled Sloan telling her how much his mom had been hurt when he'd split from his wife. This woman wore her heart on her sleeve, and part of his commitment avoidance had to do with protecting her.

"I'm not that nice," Annie teased. "We could be good friends. You're the sort of person I could grow fond of, Maggie."

She met Sloan's gaze, waiting for him to jump in and warn this woman not to get attached. That the two of them had agreed not to get serious. He remained conspicuously silent as he carefully watched to see how she would react.

"I appreciate you saying that."

"It's the truth. I tell it like I see it. And what I see is that my son hit the jackpot with you."

"We're just friends." Maggie put a finer point on it. "Friendly."

"Are we that generic?" His look and tone clearly said he was irritated at the bland description of what they were.

"Yes." She turned away from the flash of protest in his eyes. "We have pie for dessert."

Maggie knew he was thinking that he'd been in her bed and that made them more than friends. But his family didn't need to know about that, because neither of them was willing to take it to the next level.

Her problem was that since sleeping with him, she was a little less sure about *not* wanting forever after.

* * *

"Mama go bye-bye?"

"Yes, love." Maggie stooped to her daughter's level. "Mommy's going to a party."

"Me bye-bye?" Her eyes grew big, hopeful.

"Not this time, sweetie. You're going to have fun with Aunt Josie."

Her friend was standing by for a possible tantrum. "We're going to have a good time, cutie. We'll watch *Frozen* for the billionth time."

"Maybe you can talk her into a SpongeBob video."

"And hell might freeze over. No pun intended." Josie laughed. "If anyone can do it, Elsa can."

Tonight was Sydney and Burke's engagement party. She and Sloan had both been invited and were going to ride together. He'd pointed out that carpooling was the "green" thing to do. It was hard to argue with that even though she'd wanted to.

Just then he walked into the kitchen and her heart nearly stopped beating. In his dark suit, snow-white shirt and red tie he was so handsome she could hardly breathe.

Danielle toddled over to him. "You go bye-bye?"

He looked at Maggie. "How does she know? Is it the suit?"

"Must be." She smoothed the front of her black dress. It was a lace column with a peplum and cap sleeves. Simple and elegant. The four-inch heels were new, too, and the whole ensemble was way different from her everyday work clothes. "She doesn't miss much and figured something was up by the way I'm dressed."

Sloan didn't say anything. He just looked her up and down and stared. It was a good stare, the kind a man gave a woman when he enthusiastically approved of what she was wearing. And how much he wanted to take it off.

"Say something, Holden," Josie prompted.

"First I have to make sure I didn't swallow my tongue." There was a glow in his eyes. "You look beautiful."

"Thanks." Her brain was shorting out from the vibe he was giving off and heating her hormones to the boiling point. But she finally recovered enough to say, "You look very nice, too."

"Thanks."

"I guess we should go." She stooped to her daughter's level again, not easy in the tight skirt. "Give mommy a hug."

"Hug." Danielle moved into her arms and pressed her head to Maggie's chest.

"Good one, baby girl. Mommy loves you."

"'Ove you." She walked over to Sloan and held out her arms. "Hug?"

He bent down and grabbed her up, tickling until she was giggling hysterically. "'Bye, Shorty. Be nice to Josie."

Watching the big man and little girl made something shift inside Maggie. It wasn't him, but the fact that her daughter had initiated the hug. The fact that she'd automatically gone to him for a goodbye had Maggie's maternal instincts humming protectively.

"You two have fun," Josie said. "Be home by the stroke of midnight or that really expensive car he drives could turn into a pumpkin. And I don't think orange is his color."

Sloan opened the front door and settled his palm at her waist, letting her precede him. They made it outside without Danielle having a meltdown, but that was where the good news stopped. This was starting to feel an awful lot like a date. It would probably be better when they got to the party and she could mingle.

The drive didn't take long, so there wasn't too much time to fill with small talk. It also made for only a short period of trying to ignore the awareness sizzling between them. Before she knew it, Sloan drove into the Blackwater Lake Lodge parking lot and pulled into a space. He turned off the car, then got out and came around to open her door. But she'd already done it, so he offered his hand.

She took it and that was an error in judgment. His palm was warm and wide, strong and secure. The brief touch made her ache to be in his arms again.

She cleared her throat. "The lodge is lit up like this is a grand reopening or something."

"You must have seen the banner over the front door."

"It's pretty hard to miss." An uneven spot on the parking surface made her wobble in her high heels, and he took her elbow to steady her.

"You okay?"

"Fine. Just not used to these shoes."

"They're probably not very comfortable, but I meant what I said at the house. You look incredible tonight."

They were just walking under an outside light and she saw the intensity in his gaze. Knowing she was wanted was intoxicating, but too much of it impaired common sense and that was never a good thing.

"Here's the lobby." *Thank goodness*, she thought.

Automatic doors whispered open and they walked inside. There was a new wood-plank floor with an area rug and leather chairs for conversation in front of the smooth stone fireplace. Walls were newly painted a pale gold and held framed photographs of the lake and mountains. Maggie recognized the pictures from the front window of April Kennedy's photography studio.

She pointed them out to Sloan. "I like to see a business utilize local work."

"Me, too," he said. "We're doing that with labor and materials for the resort. I'll keep this in mind when we start planning the decorating phase."

There was a notice directing them to one of the lodge's banquet rooms. Walking down a cushy carpeted hallway after passing the registration desk, they heard the sound of voices drifting to them, indicating they were headed in the right direction.

They stood in the doorway and checked out the room. Tables set for dinner and covered with flowers and candles were off to the side. Overhead lights were set on romantic and contributed to that mood. People stood around talking and most had drinks in their hands. Maggie was just about to excuse herself and go mingle on her own when Sloan slid his arm around her waist.

"Let's go congratulate the happy couple," he said, indicating Burke and Sydney standing at the far end of the room.

His breath stirred her hair and tickled her ear, sending sparks dancing through her and she was simply swept along.

Sydney was already smiling happily, but it widened when they approached. She looked from Sloan to Maggie and one dark eyebrow rose. Apparently she approved of what she saw. "Well, well… So the two of you are officially an item now."

"No, we just rode together. And congratulations on your engagement." Maggie deliberately changed the subject.

"Really? Not an item?" Burke shook his cousin's hand. "I've heard rumors that your bachelormobile actually had a car seat in it. With a certain little girl strapped in."

"That's true." Sloan didn't look the least bit needled by the statement.

Maggie waited for him to clarify and when he didn't,

she said, "It's not what you're thinking. Josie couldn't watch her that day and Sloan was doing her a favor by bringing Danielle to me at the café."

"I know what you're doing," Syd said. "That was code for 'it's really new and just for us.'"

"And I think you two are high on romance and seeing it where there isn't any." Again Maggie looked at Sloan to refute the claim, but he just shrugged.

"We're very happy," Syd confirmed. "And we do want everyone else happy, too. So after the wedding, at the reception, I'll make sure to throw you the bouquet."

"That's not necessary—"

"Congrats, you two. We're going to get a drink now." Sloan took her hand in his and led her to the bar set up in a back corner. "What would you like?"

"For people to stop assuming we're together." A vision of her daughter holding out her little arms to Sloan ran through Maggie's mind. It was the cutest thing ever yet had so much potential for pain.

"I meant, what would you like to drink?"

"Wine. White."

He gave their order to the bartender and put some bills in the tip jar when the drinks were ready. Then he handed her one before picking up his scotch. He touched the rim of his tumbler to her glass. "Here's to the happy couple."

Just then Dr. and Mrs. Adam Stone walked up beside them. "And speaking of happy couples…" Jill smiled at them as if they were particularly bright. "I heard you two are dating. Adam and I think that's wonderful."

Her tall, good-looking husband nodded. "I don't listen to rumors as a rule, but you're here together, and that elevates gossip to it-must-be-true status."

"Not really," Maggie said. This man had delivered her daughter. He knew the emotional trauma and tragedy she'd gone through and the toll it had taken on her pregnancy. She couldn't let him get the wrong idea. "We carpooled tonight. That's all."

"So this isn't a date?" Jill looked disappointed.

"No, it's not." Maggie felt as if she'd just spit in Cupid's eye.

And the rest of the evening went pretty much the same way, even though she finally managed to mingle and separate herself from Sloan. His family was there and were completely charming to her again. When the party was winding down, she was more than ready to leave. They rode back to the house without either of them saying a word. He parked in the driveway beside her SUV and turned off the car. The interior was dark, the only illumination came from the front-porch light.

"You've been awfully quiet—"

"I have to tell you something—"

They both spoke at the same time and, ever the gentleman, Sloan said, "Ladies first."

"Okay." She took a deep breath. "About us... I've changed my mind. I can't take it one day at a time any more and wait to see what happens. I know what *can't* happen."

"And that is?" Wariness laced the words.

"Sleeping with you again. I can't."

"Why?"

"Everyone thinks we're dating. That we're a couple."

"What we are is no one else's business."

"That's true except when it comes to my daughter." She glanced at the driver's seat, but his expression was hidden in shadow. "She's too little to even realize this, but you're becoming a father figure to her. I first noticed it when your family came to dinner."

"What? How?"

"They were strangers invading her world and she was

uneasy about the situation. She moved to you for protection. It was instinctive." She took a breath. "And tonight when we left, she insisted on giving you a hug, too."

"It was sweet."

"Yes. And also evidence that she's getting attached to you. But you're not going to stay, and when you're gone it will break her heart."

"You can't know for sure what I'm going to do," he protested.

"I can. Your life isn't here in Blackwater Lake. If it were, you wouldn't be renting a room from me."

"That's not what this is about. You're putting up one more wall to protect yourself."

His tone challenged her to push back on that assertion, but there was no point. "You could be right, but that doesn't change anything. In spite of what the whole town thinks, we're not dating. And like you once said, it's good to have things spelled out. So I need to tell you that I'm closing the door on anything personal between us. Sleeping with you was a mistake and it can't happen again."

"That's a problem, Maggie." He shifted toward her and a shaft of porch light showed the dark passion in his eyes. "Every morning I see you at breakfast and want you. Before dinner each night I hope the wanting has gone away, but it's only stronger." He stared at her. "And I dare you to deny that you feel the same way."

"You're wrong," she lied. "But this isn't about you and me. It's about Danielle. She has to come first. I'm all she has to protect her and I will not risk her being hurt. Please, Sloan, I'm asking you to keep your distance."

"I don't think I can live in your house and honor that request." His voice was oddly calm, like the eye of a storm.

"Then, I'm going to have to ask you to leave. According to the rental agreement you signed, I have discretion to do that."

"It's a shame you feel you have to use that contract. I guess it's a good thing that Blackwater Lake Lodge is back in business. I'll move there tomorrow morning."

That was for the best, and what she'd hoped he would say. But Maggie hadn't expected the words to hit her heart like a sledgehammer.

Chapter Fourteen

The next morning Sloan booked a suite at Blackwater Lake Lodge and started packing his things. He was going to miss this room, the house—Maggie. This move didn't make him happy, and part of the reason was that *he* was always the one who walked away from a relationship, not the one who was given his walking papers. If he said that out loud, Maggie would tease him about his ego, and the thought tightened like a fist in his chest.

He wanted to fight her decision to distance herself from him. She said that was about protecting her daughter and was probably part of it, but her reasoning felt an awful lot like an excuse not to take a chance. Almost certainly, if it wasn't Danielle, Maggie would have found another reason to push him away.

His suitcase was open on the tufted stool at the foot of the king-size bed, and he threw his leather bag filled with toiletries into it. Before he could start emptying the dresser, there was a knock on the door, and hope that it was Maggie with a change of heart jumped into his mind.

But when he answered, the disappointment at finding Josie there was immediate. "Hi, what's up?"

"That's what I'm here to find out." She glanced past him to the open suitcase. "You're leaving?"

"Maggie didn't tell you?"

"No. She didn't say much at all, and you were conspicuously not present at breakfast." She shrugged. "I knew something was going on."

"I'm going, so you're right about that."

"Call me nosy, but I'm here to find out what the heck happened." She looked puzzled. "Why are you moving?"

"Maggie threw me out." That was a tad dramatic, but he was feeling that way.

"Why would she do that?" Josie's blue eyes narrowed on him. "What did you do, mister?"

"Nothing." He couldn't suppress a small smile at her tone and figured he should explain. "You sound like my mother and make me feel twelve years old again."

"That's a relief. I thought I'd lost my mojo." The older woman stood a little taller. "But something must have spooked her into evicting a stable, paying customer."

"If this was only business between us, I'd be at my office right now and not throwing my stuff into a suitcase."

Josie pushed the door wide and walked into the room. "You're saying there was something personal between you?"

"Yes." That was all he was prepared to divulge.

"I knew it!" The older woman pumped her arm in triumph.

"What exactly did you know?"

"Here's the thing. Maggie is an open book." She met his gaze, and her own had a spark of intelligence that hinted she missed very little. "You're a bit more guarded, but not much. You kissed her. I knew right away. Not because I was doing covert surveillance or anything. It was the way you acted around each other."

"How was that?"

She laughed. "Both of you worked so hard at being casual and cool. Before the kiss there was an easy give-and-take. Afterward, you acted as if an accidental touch would cause spontaneous combustion."

Eventually that was exactly what had happened, Sloan thought. And if it was up to him they would spontaneously combust again.

Often.

But after the engagement party last night, Maggie made it clear that wasn't ever going to happen. "Okay," he said grudgingly. "So we kissed."

"I also confirmed it with Maggie. I'm not proud of it, but her mother and I got her to admit it."

"So I heard." He remembered lunch with her mother.

"Maureen meant well." It was as if Josie could read his mind. "Then after a while you and Maggie sort of relaxed. Although anyone could see the sparks between you. The way you looked at her when you thought no one was watching. And Maggie did the same to you, in case you were wondering."

"I was," he admitted.

"So you care about her." She wasn't asking a question.

"Yes." Again, he wasn't prepared to say more, although he had the distinct impression this woman already knew his secrets.

"You're in love with her." Again, it wasn't a question.

Why did his feelings need a label? Couldn't they just be whatever they were? He liked spending time with Maggie. Sex was awesome and left him aching to have her again. She was beautiful, smart, hardworking, nurturing. He could go on, but that felt a lot like digging a hole he wouldn't be able to crawl out of.

And Josie was waiting for him to comment, watching him like a hawk and probably reading his mind. In case that was a power she didn't possess, he said, "I'm going to tell you what I told her brother. I've never been in love, never experienced it. So I wouldn't recognize it if it walked up and shook my hand."

"Aha," she said. "Baggage."

"Yeah." Good. She got it. Maybe she'd back off now.

"That's just an excuse for running away."

So much for cutting him some slack.

"You should be telling Maggie that, not me." He was getting irritated at taking the blame for having to move out. "I suggested to her that we take things one day at a time and see what happens."

"She didn't agree?"

"Her initial reaction was that it was sensible." He'd hated how bland she'd made the exploratory phase of a relationship sound. "But last night, just before we left, Danielle insisted on giving me a hug."

"I saw Maggie's face when that happened and hoped it wouldn't be a problem." Josie looked troubled. "I guess it was."

"Maggie said her daughter was getting attached to me and she didn't want her hurt by someone who wasn't sticking around."

"How does she know you won't?" the older woman demanded.

"That's what I said. But she refused to discuss it. Her mind was made up."

"There's more, isn't there?" She was studying him intently. "Maggie knows as well as I do that there are ways to handle Danielle's attachment if that was the only issue. But you're determined to move out. Did she ask you to?"

"Yes."

"Why?"

"She said there couldn't be anything physical between us." Sloan wasn't quite sure how she'd gotten so much information out of him, but, oddly enough, he didn't mind all that much. So what did he have to lose by telling her what she probably already knew? "I told her that every time I see her I want her again and couldn't promise that it wasn't going to happen."

"Good for you!" Then Josie frowned. "I don't understand. Why are you giving up? You wouldn't handle your business that way. What the heck is making you run away from this fight?"

Her tone clearly said she was disappointed in him, and Sloan was surprised at how much losing her good opinion bothered him. It put him even more on the defensive. "Look, Josie, you can't call me any name I haven't called myself. But this was Maggie's decision. She has enough to deal with and I don't want to make things harder for her."

"I didn't peg you for the cop-out type, Sloan."

"It's pretty easy to pass judgment when you don't have skin in the game," he said angrily.

"It is." She wasn't the least bit intimidated by his accusation and outburst. "But you're wrong. I do have a stake in this. Maggie is like the daughter I never had. Opportunities for happiness don't come along every day and second chances are even harder to find. I don't want to see Maggie blow it like I did."

"What—"

She held up a hand. "I'm not finished. You're not the only one with baggage. If you stack yours up next to hers, she'll win hands down. She lost the man she loved and is raising his child alone. That baby has to be at the top of her concern list if she considers letting a man into their lives. The thing is, you passed the test. You're terrific with Danielle, obviously a natural with kids. Danielle responded to you in the best possible way. So there's one wall down." She blew out a breath. "But now Maggie has to face the

fact that she's just plain scared to let herself care for someone again and risk getting hurt a second time."

"If I could make her take a chance, I would." Frustration laced his words and had his hands curling into fists.
"But only she can do that."

"For you she just might try," Josie said. "And if you
were here every day right under her nose, if she had to
look at you, interact with you, it would be easier to wear
down her resistance. It would be a lot harder for her to ignore her feelings."

"And if it doesn't work, where does that leave me?" he
demanded.

"You're tough. Smart. Not just a pretty face. A big boy
who would never have to say he gave up."

"What if I want to throw in the towel?"

Josie sighed. "You're hiding behind self-righteous anger
to keep the hurt from leaking through."

"My choice." His stubborn was coming out.

"It is. But sooner or later you're going to have to face
your feelings and be honest about them."

"Maybe." The bullheaded streak wasn't going to let him
admit she had a point.

"Or you could decide to continue ignoring the obvious."

"There are benefits," he maintained.

Josie nodded as if to say she felt sorry for him. She
smiled sadly and met his gaze. "I'm going to miss watching TV with you."

"Come to the lodge. The suite has a TV."

"It won't be the same." She walked over and hugged
him. "Goodbye, Sloan."

"Take care of her, Josie."

She nodded, then left him to his packing.

He threw things into the suitcase and wallowed in his
self-righteous indignation. When there was nothing left to

pack, the bubble of anger and resentment popped. It was time to face walking away from Maggie and this brief but wonderful glimpse into a life that could have been everything he'd ever wanted. Josie's words drifted through his mind about being a quitter. They stung, but he didn't see any future in taking his head out of the sand.

The problem with leaving it there was that it left his ass exposed.

Two days. Forty-eight hours.

Maggie couldn't stop herself from marking time in terms of before and after Sloan. It had been two days since he'd moved out of her house. Correction: her B and B. He'd been a paying guest and it wasn't supposed to get personal. So she'd fixed the problem and now he was gone. If only her house would stop feeling so empty without him in it.

Speaking of empty—her stomach growled, a reminder that she hadn't eaten lunch and it was nearly two o'clock in the afternoon. Food hadn't been high on her list for the past couple of days, but she needed something or she'd get sick. That wasn't an option.

She left her office and went downstairs to the café. The lunch rush was over and only a few customers were in the place. Lucy was ringing up a couple's bill, and after paying it they left. She picked up the half-filled coffeepot and strolled over to the table where the lone customer sat and topped off his mug. There was a flirty expression on her partner's face, then Maggie noticed that the guy was very cute. Brown hair, blue eyes and broad shoulders—a triple threat. He also had a nice smile.

When she finally looked up and spotted Maggie, Lucy waved her over. "I was wondering when you'd surface for lunch."

"I guess that would be now." Maggie shrugged.

"Have you two met?" Lucy indicated the thirtysomething man she'd been chatting up. "He works for Sloan."

"We haven't run into each other." Although just hearing Sloan's name made Maggie feel as if she'd run into a brick wall. "I'm Maggie Potter."

"Dalton Sparks. It's nice to meet you, Maggie." He shook her hand.

"I was just telling Dalton about all the fantastic things Blackwater Lake has to offer," her partner gushed.

"It's a pretty little place," he responded, his eyes never leaving Lucy.

"It would be hard to find more spectacular scenery anywhere." The woman was practically purring. She rested the half-full pot on the table. "And you can't beat the people. Salt of the earth. Best anywhere. Friendly, hardworking. Always there if you need them."

Maggie wondered if her friend should be on the town's tourism and public relations committee. She was doing quite a sales pitch on the man. It was obvious because everything she'd said was what Maggie would have pitched to Sloan in order to talk him into staying. But she never had.

There were times when Maggie envied her partner. By taking a break from men, and apparently no emotional baggage, Lucy could be carefree. The only person she had to think about was herself. If she met a good-looking man there was nothing to stop her from pulling out all the stops. Maggie could barely remember a time when she didn't have to consider a little girl, whose welfare came first. The love for her child was tremendously big and all consuming, but it didn't quite fill up the lonely places inside her, the places that missed Sloan.

"How do you like Blackwater Lake?" she asked the newcomer to town.

"Seems like a great place," he said.

"Do you enjoy working here?" Lucy wanted to know.

"If you'd asked me that two days ago I'd have answered yes without hesitation. But my boss has developed a bad case of surly and it's showing no sign of letting up any-time soon."

Two days? That was when Maggie had asked him to leave the bed-and-breakfast. It probably wasn't a coinci-dence. Part of her wanted to believe he was crabby be-cause he missed her, too. The practical part shut down that thought. And before she could figure out how to delicately phrase a question, the café's front door opened. Automati-cally she turned to look and saw her brother, Brady, walk in. He glanced around, then spotted her and came over.

"Ladies. How's it going, Dalton?" He obviously had met the man who worked with Sloan.

Dalton stood and shook hands. "Good to see you, Brady. I was just saying that things could be better."

"What's wrong?"

"Sloan. His attitude stinks. It's as if someone told him he has to paint the outside of the new resort pink or some-thing." Dalton shook his head. "And speaking of work, I better get back to it. You know what they say about pok-ing an angry bear."

"I'll ring up your check." Lucy led him over to the cash register.

Maggie watched the other woman smile up at the new guy, then met her brother's gaze. "Hi, there. Are you here for lunch?"

"Yeah."

"It's kind of late."

"I've been kind of busy," he said.

"Me, too. I just came down for a quick bite myself."

"Good. Join me," he invited. "I hate to eat alone."

"Since when?" she asked. "After you met a computer, you made a friend."

"Very funny. Although kind of true." He grinned. "Maybe falling in love with Olivia changed me for the better."

"Definitely better. You had nowhere to go but up," Maggie teased. She led him to a table for two by the front window and they sat down across from each other. "That's the thing. Because she's your executive assistant you took her for granted. You took advantage of her for years. But I don't think you suddenly fell for her. You just always loved her."

"I see that now. But it wasn't until she gave me notice that she was quitting and leaving town for another job that I started to pay closer attention."

"She shook you up."

His eyes narrowed. "As I recall, you had a little to do with that."

"Oh, who can remember." Maggie waved her hand dismissively.

"I do, as a matter of fact. It was your idea for her to quit."

"She tried to give her notice more than once, but you dangled more money in front of her. All she wanted was for you to love her."

Brady's expression turned serious. "I don't know what I would have done without her."

"You would have gone after her. Just like you did when she took that trip to Florida." Maggie grabbed two menus stacked beside the salt-and-pepper shakers and handed one to him. "Olivia said you proposed to her right there on the beach."

"What can I say? I'm spontaneous. A man of action."

Maggie scoffed. "It only took you five years."

"I had issues," he defended.

Lucy walked over to them, order pad in hand. "Hi, Brady. How are you?"

"Good. You?"

"Can't complain." She glanced over her shoulder to the door where Dalton had just exited. "I have to say that the resort project is bringing in a lot of interesting men to deepen the dating pool."

As far as Maggie was concerned, the pool could be a puddle and that would be deep enough for her. Her experience with Sloan had shown her the wisdom of not dipping her toe in the water. If only she'd listened to her own warnings and stuck to her guns when she'd blathered to him about not inviting him into her bedroom. Now she missed him so much she ached from it.

"So what'll you two have?" Lucy asked.

"Hamburger." Brady hadn't even looked at the menu.

"If that's what you had your heart set on, you should have gone to the Grizzly Bear Diner," Maggie said.

"Excuse me," Lucy objected. "But in Building a Business 101, it says that you should encourage people to come into your establishment, not send them to the competition."

"He's not people. He's my brother. And he doesn't pay anyway," Maggie reminded her.

"Wait a second. I'm not a freeloader," he protested. "I did your website at no charge. And I'm here because the beef you serve is grass fed and comes with a side of field greens or fruit. Organic and healthy. My woman will be so proud."

"Okay, then." Lucy looked at her. "Maggie?"

"Vegetable soup."

"And?" Lucy and Brady said together.

"That's it. I'm not very hungry." Her stomach growled

in spite of the knot that told her she would have trouble getting the soup down.

"I'll throw half a tuna-salad sandwich on the plate." Lucy turned away.

"She's a gigantic pain in the neck," Maggie said fondly.

"And she cares about you," her brother reminded her. "A lot of people do. So what's wrong, Maggie?"

Ah. This was why he hadn't gone to the diner. There was an ulterior motive for showing up at the Harvest Café.

"Nothing's wrong. I'm fine."

"Let's leave that for now. I'll come back to it because you're not fine." Brady met her gaze. "But it's important for you to know that Sloan has been like the walking dead since the night of Burke and Sydney's engagement party. And from what Dalton just said and my own observations, it's clear something happened between you two that night, because the rumor is that the next morning he moved into Blackwater Lake Lodge."

"He did."

Brady waited for more. When it didn't come, he prodded, "And?"

"Nothing. He moved out of the bed-and-breakfast."

"Why?"

Maggie recognized the stubborn look on his face and knew he wouldn't let this go unless she explained. "I asked him to leave."

"Why?" Then he frowned. "Did he do something?"

The only thing he did was be his charming, irresistible self, she thought. "Nothing like you're thinking. He's great with Danielle, and that's a problem."

He stared at her for a moment, then shook his head. "I'm not seeing the issue."

"He's not staying and she's getting attached to him."

"Her? Or you?" Brady asked.

"She's a little girl. I'm not. I understand that he's temporary but Danielle doesn't. I have to protect her."

"Really?" One dark eyebrow rose. "Or is it yourself you're protecting?"

"She's my number one priority," Maggie snapped. "It's my job to raise her the way Danny would have."

"I get that. But raising your daughter doesn't mean you can't have a life, too." Brady reached across the table and covered her hand with his own. "It's obvious to anyone who sees you and Sloan together that you care about each other."

It would be so much easier if she didn't like him so much. Her determination to keep him at a distance had been no match for the power of her attraction to him.

"Brady, if you don't mind, I would rather not talk about this."

He squeezed her fingers then let go of her hand. "I just have one more thing to say."

"It better be short and sweet."

"You once lectured me about getting over loss, moving on and making the most of every day. It's about time you took your own advice."

"It's not that easy," she protested.

"That's where you're wrong. Falling in love is easy. It's taking a leap of faith that's hard. Trust me, I know. And you're the one who gave me the kick in the butt I needed to get out of my own way."

"Look, Brady, I must have sounded like an annoying know-it-all. I didn't mean to. But you and Olivia have known each other forever. It was a very different situation between the two of you. Mine is complicated—"

He held up a hand to stop her. "Don't apologize. Not to me. I couldn't be more grateful that you made me see the light. I love Olivia more than anything and I'm grateful for every single second that we spend together. I'm deliriously happy with her. And that's why I'm here. I want you to be deliriously happy, too."

"I know." She tried to smile but tears were right there. It wasn't so easy putting on a brave front to someone who knew you almost as well as you knew yourself. "Thanks for caring about me."

"And that's code for you're finished with this conversation." He sighed. "Just keep in mind that cowards always have regrets."

"Okay, then. Good talk, Brady."

Not.

Coward? That seemed a little harsh. *Don't sugarcoat it*, Maggie thought. *Tell me how you really feel.* And that was the problem. Feelings. She didn't want them.

Not ever again.

But she didn't know how to make them go away.

Chapter Fifteen

Maggie came home from work, parked in front of the house and tried her new attitude, which was to feel nothing at all. Normally spending time with her brother lifted her spirits, but not today. And her spirits would sink even further when she walked in the door. That was all about the fact that Sloan had done as she'd asked and no longer lived under her roof. She looked at the place and couldn't help thinking it looked as sad as she felt.

She braced herself for the overpowering emptiness waiting for her inside. That morning Josie had said she wouldn't be there for dinner, and Danielle was with her mom, due here shortly. But right this minute the house was deserted. Sloan was never coming back, and in spite of trying to feel nothing, Maggie swore she could feel her heart crack.

She exited the car and walked to the rear to retrieve the two small bags of groceries she'd picked up on the way home. Milk, bread, fruit, eggs and her daughter's favorite cookies. It made Maggie probably the world's worst mother, but she'd been a little lax with the cookie rules in the past couple of days.

After unlocking the front door, Maggie went inside and turned on lights as she made her way to the kitchen, then settled the bags along with her purse on the island. She busied herself putting groceries away. Busy was good. It would keep her from missing his cheerful, charming disposition along with the broad shoulders and brown eyes. Not to mention her own sense of security and support. If she needed him he'd be there—or he would have been if she hadn't thrown him out.

The sound of a car door slamming drifted to her. "Oh, thank God."

Moments later the bell rang and the door opened, followed by her mother's voice. "Maggie?"

"In the kitchen."

"Mama!" Danielle's little feet sounded on the wood floor.

Maggie went down on one knee and opened her arms, grabbing that little warm body in a hug and holding her close. "Hi, baby girl. Did you have fun with Grandma?"

"Book. 'Bary."

"Library," her mother enunciated. "I took her for story time. We were in the car anyway and it was easier for me to drop her off than have you pick her up."

Maybe that was the reason her mom had called and said she'd drop Danielle off, but Maggie wasn't so sure. "I hate to have you go out of your way, Mom. You're doing me a favor."

"It's not a favor. I love spending time with my grandchild. You know that." Maureen watched the little girl toddle toward the stairs, obviously calling for someone. "What is she doing?"

Maggie sighed and met her mom's gaze. "She's looking for Sloan. Been doing it since he left. She's too little to understand why he's not here."

"That makes two of us. I don't understand and I'm a lot older than she is."

Maggie caught up with her daughter before she could climb the stairs. "It's complicated, Mom."

"I've got time." Maureen took off her sweater and hung it on one of the bar stools at the island and set her purse on the seat. "Explain it to me."

Maggie put her squirming-to-get-down daughter in the high chair and warmed some cut-up chicken and green beans, then put it on the tray. Danielle instantly grabbed a piece in her chubby fingers. She put it in her mouth, then took another, in a not very ladylike way. One of these days, they would work on manners.

The explain-it-to-me remark had been a clue, and now Maggie knew for sure that dropping Danielle off at home was a contrived excuse. Her mother's real purpose was to interfere in her personal life. "You talked to Brady, didn't you?"

"What makes you say that?" her mom hedged.

"Oh, please. Nothing happens in this family that doesn't get relayed to all at light speed." She rested her hands on her hips. "He came into the café for lunch today and I explained everything to him. I'm sure he shared the high points with you."

"He did." Her mother sighed. "But the explanation doesn't make sense to me."

"I can't help that. It makes perfect sense to me." *Mostly.*

"I'll admit to having doubts about Sloan at first. After all, he can't help that he's handsome and wealthy and women are drawn to him like—well, the nicest metaphor is bees to honey."

Maggie wished she was the exceptional woman who successfully ignored his appeal, but unfortunately she'd succumbed. And it wasn't about those qualities. She'd been drawn to them as much as the fact that he was a really good guy. "What's your point, Mom?"

"My point is that he proved me wrong. He manned up and came to my house for lunch. He ate quiche and said he enjoyed it." Her mom took a breath. "And while he was being a real man and choking down that quiche, I grilled him like raw meat. About his women. He said the stories were exaggerated and he wasn't that guy. I believed him when he told me he would never deliberately hurt you, that you're a special woman. It shows he has good taste."

It was the "deliberately" part, Maggie thought. He might not mean for it to happen, but as soon as you let someone into your heart you left yourself open to hurt. "You saw the way Danielle was looking for him. She was getting used to him. What happens to her when he leaves town? I won't let her be hurt."

"Oh, Maggie—" Her mom pressed her lips together. "A mother's job is to protect her babies, but we can't do that all the time. If it was possible, I'd have done that for you. With Danny—"

"I know."

"The only positive thing I can say is that what doesn't kill you makes you stronger. A cliché, I know, but that doesn't make it any less true. You're strong and you have to move on with your life."

"I have."

"You're raising a child and working at your business." Maureen shook her head. "But you have no joy in a personal relationship with a man. I saw a flash of it when Sloan was here, but it's gone now."

"Mom—"

"I hear a patronizing tone and we'll nip that in the bud." Speaking of flashes, there was one in her mother's eyes. "No one knows you as well as your mother. On top of that, the two of us are members of an exclusive club no woman wants to belong to. We're widows. We both lost the man we loved. And it sucks. I know. I recognized your pain when you got the news and the light went out of your eyes. I saw when it came back on—when Sloan was here."

"I don't want Danielle to get attached to him," Maggie said stubbornly.

"You mean the way you were to your dad?" A sad look slid into her mom's eyes.

"Yeah." Maggie would never forget the shock of her father's sudden heart attack, the pain of finding out he was gone.

"You were older when he died, but there were still things you missed out on. Seeing the look of amazement in your father's eyes when you were all dressed up for your first formal dance. You didn't have the man whose mere presence in the house told all those boys who came calling not to mess with his daughter." There was a hitch in her voice before she said, "Giving you away on your wedding day."

"Danielle won't miss what she never had," Maggie protested.

"That's just it. She could have all of that. She could have a man in her life to be the best kind of role model. She wouldn't be missing Sloan now if he hadn't shown that he was ready and up to the challenge of being a father. The kind of man who would navigate the complex world of car seats and strollers to help you out is looking for family. He's ready to support you because he cares about you and your daughter. But you have to meet him halfway, baby girl."

"Oh, Mom—"

"Cookie?"

Maggie looked at her daughter's messy high chair tray. There was food sticking to it and some on the floor. Guessing the little girl had consumed enough, she gave her a cookie from the brand-new box sitting on the island. Happily, Danielle shoved it into her mouth.

Maggie looked back at her own mother and recognized hope and pain in her expression. "I don't know if I can move on. You never did."

"I would have—if I'd met anyone who made me want to," Maureen admitted.

"Josie lost her husband and she hasn't moved on." Maggie was grasping at straws to make an argument, support her decision to push Sloan away.

"Are you sure about that?"

Something in her mother's voice got her attention. "Is she seeing someone? Who?"

"You don't think she went all that way to the hospital in Copper Hill when Hank Fletcher had his heart attack and only stayed there just for his daughter, Kim, do you?"

"She's dating the sheriff?"

"Hank is a widower. And technically he's not the sheriff right now, what with being on medical leave. But, yes. They have been discreetly hanging out, or whatever it's called these days." Her mother smiled. "She's moving on."

"I'm happy for her."

"Me, too." She released a big sigh. "I know what loneliness feels like. No one knows better than me that it takes a toll. I can see what it's doing to you, Maggie, and it breaks my heart. Especially when there's a chance to change it."

"Mom, I—"

"Get back out there, Maggie. Sloan is a good man. But if you don't love him, that's a different story."

"It's not that," she whispered. "I'm afraid."

Maureen moved close and wrapped Maggie in her arms. "I know, baby girl. I get it."

"What if I lose him, too, Mom?"

"What if you don't?" There was steel in her mother's

voice. "The choices you make in life don't come with a money-back guarantee. You can put a wall around your heart to protect it, but that's not really living. Or you can take a chance and make the choice to live every day to the fullest."

Maggie's eyes filled with tears. "What if I blew my chance?"

"Well—" Her mother's expression turned fiercely protective. "You know what love feels like and I expect you would recognize it if that's what you have with Sloan. This may come as a surprise, but he can't read your mind. If you love him, you have to tell him."

"What if—"

"No. Don't borrow trouble. You tell him what's on your mind. It will either work out or it won't. But you'll never have to wonder what might have been. You'll never have to say, 'if only.'"

Maggie nodded. "Good talk, Mom."

And this time she meant those words with all her heart.

Later, after putting Danielle to bed, Maggie waited for Josie to come home. She was hoping her friend would babysit because there was something important she had to do.

Unable to sit still, she paced the length of the house, rehearsing what she wanted to say. A jumble of thoughts went through her mind but she couldn't pull them together. Then finally she heard a car pull into the driveway, and at this time of night it wouldn't be anyone but Josie. Her friend always used the front door instead of the outside stairs and Maggie waited for her to come in.

Josie unlocked the door and opened it. When she saw Maggie, her eyes widened. "Is everything okay?"

"Yes. Fine." If you didn't factor in that she'd been a stubborn coward. "I was just wondering if you could keep an eye on Danielle for me."

"Of course. I can give her a bath—"

"She's in bed already. Mom wore her out today at the library and she didn't have a nap." Maggie twisted her fingers together. "If you could just listen for her I'd really appreciate it."

"Sure." Josie looked at her watch. "It's after eight. Must be pretty important."

"I have an—errand."

"Kind of late, isn't it?" There was a knowing look on her friend's face. "This errand isn't by any chance the handsome and charming man who, until recently, lived here, is it?"

Maggie sighed. It was too much to hope that she could pull this off without anyone else knowing about it. In her defense, it was difficult to pull off a covert operation when you had a two-year-old. But Josie was guessing.

"Why would you think that?"

"I talked to your mother." Josie's expression grew firm. "Before you get huffy, you should know that she's worried about you. She needed to unburden herself to someone."

Maggie fought a smile. "Unburdening oneself sounds so much more tasteful than gossiping."

"It does. Thank you for noticing. But it's also true. Maureen could see how distracted and unhappy you've been and, frankly, I did, too."

"I didn't mean to worry anyone."

"It comes with the territory. We love you." Her friend turned serious. "Just keep in mind that he was hurt and angry when he left here."

"You talked to him?"

"Yes."

"So am I wasting my time? Maybe he won't see me—"

Josie held up a hand. "I'm sure he's cooled off by now. And just remember, if you don't try, you'll never forgive yourself."

"Yeah. That seems to be the majority opinion." Her wise family had made her see the truth of it. And she knew from personal experience that what might have been was more painful than facing up to what was going on right now.

"Okay, then. And before you leave, I just want to say that you need to remember when he left here he was running away, too."

"From what?"

"That's something you need to ask him. But trust me, honey, it's an even playing field."

"Okay." She hugged her friend. "Thanks."

"Anytime. Now go run your errand. And put on your raincoat. It's drizzly and cold outside."

Maggie did as ordered, then grabbed her keys and purse and drove to Blackwater Lake Lodge, where her "errand" was currently residing. *Nervous* didn't adequately describe how she was feeling. Her nerves had nerves. And it would be ridiculously easy to turn the car around and go home. But Brady and her mom were right. She'd lost her husband in a situation that was completely beyond her control. With Sloan... Well, she would regret it forever if she didn't at least talk to him one last time.

She exited her car and headed for the lodge's bright lights. When the lobby doors automatically whispered open, she stopped short. Obviously she hadn't thought this completely through.

She had no idea what room he was staying in.

As the owner of a B and B, she was well aware of a guest's safety and privacy rights. Now that she was here, there was only one thing she could do.

She walked up to the reception desk and smiled at the young man there, whose name tag said Ron.

"Hi, Ron. I'm here to see one of your guests. Sloan Holden." The guy looked uncomfortable and started to say something, but her patience and nerves were on thin ice. She interrupted. "I'm aware that you're not permitted to give out room numbers. I was hoping you could call and just let him know Maggie Potter is here to see him."

"Of course." Ron looked relieved that she didn't push the issue.

Maggie's heart pounded as he picked up the phone, dialed and waited for an answer. She pulled the belt a little tighter on her water-resistant coat with sweaty hands and realized her pulse was racing. How had all those women sneaked into his room and stripped naked to wait in his bed? It would take more nerve than she had. Obviously she wasn't cut out to be a stalker groupie.

Finally she heard Ron say, "Yes, sir. I'll send her right up." The guy replaced the phone and said, "He's in the suite on the top floor."

"What's the room number?"

"He said he'll be waiting for you."

Maggie wanted to grill this young man like raw hamburger. Did Sloan sound happy that she was here? Angry? Or worse—annoyed? There was only one way to find out and she wasn't hiding from it anymore. She braced herself and stiffened her spine, then walked around the corner to the elevator and rode it to the top floor of the lodge.

When the doors opened, she saw an arrow on the wall directing visitors to the rooms. She followed the hall to the suite and found out why she didn't need to know a number.

Sloan was standing in the doorway.

Maggie's breath caught and she couldn't look at him hard enough. It felt like a lifetime since she'd last seen him. The sleeves of his white shirt were rolled up and his gray slacks were wrinkled, indicating a lot of sitting behind a desk. His dark hair looked as if he'd dragged his fingers through it countless times. Most of all, there were lines in his face, deeper than she'd ever noticed. He looked tired and she badly wanted to smooth the weariness away.

"Maggie." His voice wasn't as enthusiastic as she would have liked.

"Hi." She met his gaze. "I thought about being naked under this coat, but showing up here at all makes me feel really vulnerable."

When he didn't say anything, she started talking. "You were right about me. I was carrying around a lot of baggage about my husband's death and subconsciously felt it was wrong for me to be happy. Survivor's guilt and regrets that he died before his daughter was born. That makes me sound a little crazy, but it's really more complicated than that. I was afraid to let anyone in. I was terrified of caring again and being hurt. And not just me this time. Danielle, too. She wouldn't miss her father because she never had a chance to know him. But she was getting to know you.

"What if you left me? She would be devastated, too." Maggie took a deep breath and prayed that he would say something. But he just stared at her, intensity darkening his eyes. Fortunately she was almost finished, because he probably wanted her gone.

"I tried so hard to keep you out. For Danielle's sake, but mostly for me. The thing is, I just couldn't keep you out. I fell in love with you, Sloan."

Maggie looked at him and waited. And waited some more. Then her heart squeezed tight to hold back the pain.

"Okay, then. I'll take your silence as a sign that you aren't on the same page. I'm sorry I bothered you." She stepped back and started to turn away.

Sloan reached out, took her arm to stop her and simply said, "Stay."

"Why? You have nothing to say to me."

With his index finger, he traced the collar of her rain-coat. "I just got an image of you naked under this coat and words failed me."

"I'm not sure I believe that." But hope blossomed in-side her. "You're probably the most smooth-talking man I've ever met."

"Normally I am, but not where you're concerned." He pulled her into the suite and closed the door. "If you hadn't come to me, I was going to you. Prepared to wear you down with sheer persistence."

"Josie said you left because you were running away. Why?"

"I didn't want to be hurt. Just like you." He sighed. "But the longer I was away, the more I knew I had to fight for you. I couldn't let you go without trying."

"Really?"

"God's honest truth." He curled his fingers around her arms. "I love you, Maggie. Pretty much since I showed up on your doorstep. You're everything I ever wanted and thought I'd never find. If I'd known my dream was here in Blackwater Lake, I would have come to town sooner."

Happiness flooded through her. "I think things hap-pened exactly the way they were supposed to. I might not have been ready for love before now. And missing out on loving you would have broken my heart. Sooner? Later?" She shrugged. "It doesn't matter because we have the rest of our lives to be together."

"Starting now," he said, his gaze on hers. "I want a family with you. I love that little girl of yours as if she was my own."

"She's missed you terribly. Keeps trying to go upstairs to find you." She smiled. "It was watching her turn to you like she would a father that freaked me out."

"Don't be," he pleaded. "I'll be the best father to her that I know how to be. Marry me, Maggie."

"You're willing to give up your standing as one of the world's most eligible bachelors?" She grinned up at him.

"More than you will ever know," he said fervently. "Marry me."

"You're not going to miss the women showing up in your room?"

"The only woman I'd miss if she didn't show up in my room is you. Please say you'll marry me, Maggie."

"On one condition."

"Anything," he said.

"You'll move back into the house." She met his gaze. "Into my room."

"Wow. You drive a hard bargain." He grinned. "Done. Now please put me out of my misery, because I want more than anything to marry you."

"Yes," she said.

He breathed a sigh of relief and pulled her against him. "Is Josie with Danielle?"

"She is."

"Do you think she would mind giving her breakfast in the morning?" There was a gleam in his eyes that was both passion and promise.

"I think that could be arranged. Why?"

"Because I'd really like to unbutton that coat and find you naked."

"All night?"

"And for the rest of our lives," he said.

And so much for their bargain not to get personal. This one worked for her so much better.

* * * * *

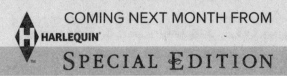

COMING NEXT MONTH FROM

HARLEQUIN

SPECIAL EDITION

Available January 19, 2016

#2455 FORTUNE'S PERFECT VALENTINE

The Fortunes of Texas: All Fortune's Children • by Stella Bagwell

Computer programmer Vivian Blair believes the secret to a successful marriage is compatibility, while her boss, Wes Robinson, thinks passion's the only ingredient in a romance. When she develops a matchmaking app and challenges him to use it, which one will prove the other right...and find true love?

#2456 DR. FORGET-ME-NOT

Matchmaking Mamas • by Marie Ferrarella

When Dr. Mitchell Stewart begins volunteering at a shelter alongside teacher Melanie McAdams, he falls head-over-stethoscope for the blonde beauty. Once burned in love, Melanie's not looking for forever, even in the capable arms of a man like Mitchell. Can the medic's bedside manner convince Melanie to open her heart to a happy ending?

#2457 A SOLDIER'S PROMISE

Wed in the West • by Karen Templeton

Former soldier Levi Talbot returns to Whispering Pines, New Mexico, to make good on his promise to look after his best friend's family. The last thing he expects is to fall in love with his pal's widow, Valerie Lopez. Now, Levi's in for the battle of his life—one he's determined to win.

#2458 THE DOCTOR'S VALENTINE DARE

Rx for Love • by Cindy Kirk

Dr. Noah Anson's can-do attitude has always met with success, both professionally and personally. But when he runs up against the most stubborn woman in Jackson Hole, Josie Campbell, nothing goes the way he planned. It will take a whole lotta lovin' to win Josie's heart...and that's what he's determined to do!

#2459 WAKING UP WED

Sugar Falls, Idaho • by Christy Jeffries

When old friends Kylie Chatterson and Drew Gregson wake up in Las Vegas with matching wedding bands, all they want to say is "I don't!" But when they're forced to live together and care for Drew's twin nephews, they realize married life might be the happy ending they'd both always dreamed of.

#2460 A VALENTINE FOR THE VETERINARIAN

Paradise Animal Clinic • by Katie Meyer

Single mom and veterinarian Cassie Marshall swore off men for good when her ex walked out on her. But Alex Santiago, new to Paradise and its police department, and his adorable K9 partner melt Cassie's heart. This Valentine's Day, can the doc and the deputy create a forever family?

YOU CAN FIND MORE INFORMATION ON UPCOMING HARLEQUIN® TITLES, FREE EXCERPTS AND MORE AT WWW.HARLEQUIN.COM.

HSECNM0116

REQUEST YOUR FREE BOOKS!

2 FREE NOVELS PLUS 2 FREE GIFTS!

(H) HARLEQUIN®

SPECIAL EDITION

Life, Love & Family

YES! Please send me 2 FREE Harlequin® Special Edition novels and my 2 FREE gifts (gifts are worth about $10). After receiving them, if I don't wish to receive any more books, I can return the shipping statement marked "cancel." If I don't cancel, I will receive 6 brand-new novels every month and be billed just $4.74 per book in the U.S. or $5.49 per book in Canada. That's a savings of at least 12% off the cover price! It's quite a bargain! Shipping and handling is just 50¢ per book in the U.S. and 75¢ per book in Canada.* I understand that accepting the 2 free books and gifts places me under no obligation to buy anything. I can always return a shipment and cancel at any time. Even if I never buy another book, the two free books and gifts are mine to keep forever.

235/335 HDN GH3Z

Name	(PLEASE PRINT)	
Address		Apt. #
City	State/Prov.	Zip/Postal Code

Signature (if under 18, a parent or guardian must sign)

Mail to the **Reader Service:**
IN U.S.A.: P.O. Box 1867, Buffalo, NY 14240-1867
IN CANADA: P.O. Box 609, Fort Erie, Ontario L2A 5X3

Want to try two free books from another line?
Call 1-800-873-8635 or visit www.ReaderService.com.

* Terms and prices subject to change without notice. Prices do not include applicable taxes. Sales tax applicable in N.Y. Canadian residents will be charged applicable taxes. Offer not valid in Quebec. This offer is limited to one order per household. Not valid for current subscribers to Harlequin Special Edition books. All orders subject to credit approval. Credit or debit balances in a customer's account(s) may be offset by any other outstanding balance owed by or to the customer. Please allow 4 to 6 weeks for delivery. Offer available while quantities last.

Your Privacy—The Reader Service is committed to protecting your privacy. Our Privacy Policy is available online at www.ReaderService.com or upon request from the Reader Service.

We make a portion of our mailing list available to reputable third parties that offer products we believe may interest you. If you prefer that we not exchange your name with third parties, or if you wish to clarify or modify your communication preferences, please visit us at www.ReaderService.com/consumerschoice or write to us at Reader Service Preference Service, P.O. Box 9062, Buffalo, NY 14240-9062. Include your complete name and address.

HSE15

SPECIAL EXCERPT FROM

♦ H HARLEQUIN®
™

SPECIAL EDITION

*Dr. Mitchell Stewart experiences unusual symptoms
when he meets beautiful volunteer Melanie McAdams.
His heart's pounding and his pulse is racing...could this
be love? But it'll take some work to show commitment-
shy Melanie he means forever...*

*Read on for a sneak preview of
DR. FORGET-ME-NOT, the latest volume in*
Marie Ferrarella's
MATCHMAKING MAMAS miniseries.

Closing her eyes for a moment, Melanie sighed. She had
no answer for the taunting voice in her head. No theory
to put forth to satisfy her conscience and this sudden,
unannounced huge wave of guilt that had just washed
over her like a tsunami after a 9.9 earthquake. And, like
it or not, that was what Mitch's kiss had felt like to her,
an earthquake. A great, big, giant earthquake and she
wasn't even sure if the ground beneath her feet hadn't
disappeared altogether, thanks to liquefaction. She felt
just that unsteady.

She'd stayed sitting down even after Mitch had left
the room.

*Damn it, the man kissed you. He didn't perform a
lobotomy on you with his tongue. Get a grip and get back
to work. Life goes on, remember?*

That was just the problem. Life went on. The love
of her life had been taken away ten months ago and for
some reason, life still went on.

Squaring her shoulders, she slid off the makeshift exam table, otherwise known in her mind as the scene of the crime, tested the steadiness of her legs and, once that was established, left the room.

Whether Melanie liked it or not, there was still a lot of work to do, and it wasn't going to get done by itself.

She had almost managed to talk herself into a neutral, rational place as she made her way past the dining hall, which, when Mitch was here, still served as his unofficial waiting room. That was when she heard Mitch call out to her.

"Melanie, I need you."

Everything inside her completely froze.

It was the same outside. It was as if her legs, after working fine all these years, had suddenly forgotten how to move and take her from point A to point B.

She had to have heard him wrong.

The Dr. Mitchell Stewart she had come to know these past few weeks would have never uttered those words to anyone, least of all to her.

And would the Mitchell Stewart you think you know so well have singed off your lips like that?

Don't miss
DR. FORGET-ME-NOT
by USA TODAY *bestselling author Marie Ferrarella,*
available February 2016 wherever
Harlequin® Special Edition books and ebooks are sold.

www.Harlequin.com

HSEEXP0116

HARLEQUIN®

A *Romance* FOR EVERY MOOD™

Love the Harlequin book you just read?

Your opinion matters.

Review this book on your favorite
book site, review site, blog or your own
social media properties and share
your opinion with other readers!

Be sure to connect with us at:
Harlequin.com/Newsletters
Facebook.com/HarlequinBooks
Twitter.com/HarlequinBooks

HARLEQUIN®

A *Romance* FOR EVERY MOOD™

JUST CAN'T GET ENOUGH?

Join our social communities
and talk to us online.

You will have access to the latest
news on upcoming titles and special
promotions, but most importantly,
you can talk to other fans about your
favorite Harlequin reads.

Harlequin.com/Community

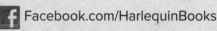

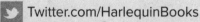